HEAVEN

Michael C. Doyle

Heaven

Published by The Conrad Press in the United Kingdom 2021

Tel: +44(0)1227 472 874
www.theconradpress.com
info@theconradpress.com

ISBN 978-1-913567-56-9

Typesetting and Cover Design by:
Charlotte Mouncey, www.bookstyle.co.uk

The Conrad Press logo was designed by Maria Priestley.

Printed and bound in Great Britain by Clays Ltd, Elcograf S.p.A.

To my wife Sharon

Chapter 1

Afterlife

The sun was shining through the trees like a rainbow of light and it dazzled me as I walked through the forest. I sat down on the grass and took a rest. I thought about heaven and what it would be like. What if an afterlife does not exist at all? Would I wake up in heaven - or cease to exist?

I lay mediating for a long time and then suddenly I felt as my soul was about to leave my body as though a surge of energy, an omnipotent force, was about to lift my soul and raise it up. All of a sudden my soul hovered above me, it was beyond time. I was there in a timeless state fully conscious and looking down on my body.

It was perfect bliss, now I thought.

Now trials and tribulations of the past life were gone. I was on a spiritual journey where souls merge to become one with God and eternity. My soul was departing from my mortal body as I lay on the grass and now for the first time I was about to be judged by my Maker.

My life was recalled back to my childhood. I had not been to confession since I was in the monastery, and now the Lord summons me on Judgement Day, what chance of me going to heaven, a sinner!

Then out of nowhere there was a blinding light and there appeared before me the archangel Raphael, who said he was taking me to the Judgement Hall, where the verdict would be announced.

'God is merciful,' said Raphael. 'Trust in God.'

Then he took me up into the clouds in a never-ending tunnel of light until there was a golden palace full of angels, who beckoned me into the Judgement Hall. It was there I met the Lord.

I stood trembling before Christ, not knowing what I would say or what He would ask me about my earthly life and my sins. He studied the official document given to him by the archangel Michael and without hesitation He pronounced his verdict.

'You have come before the Heavenly Court on Judgement Day. Judging by what you done, you were twice married and then went with prostitutes. Full of contrition, you entered the monastery. Why did you leave?'

I cried out: 'I am not worthy to be a monk. I am a wretched sinner, but I implore you, while I grieve about my sinful life, I pray will have mercy, Lord.'

The Lord looked at me, and pointed a finger, saying: 'You should go down to purgatory. There you will have time to think about what you did in the earthly life and then you will be brought before the Judgement Hall to await the final sentence. Go now and repent.'

On hearing that I went away dejected. Purgatory was a temporary suffering but it was more painful and terrible than this earthly life could bear.

Archangel Raphael took me to the border between heaven and purgatory, an unending chasm. I stood at the abyss pondering my fate not knowing whether to live or die. The next thing the archangel told me to take the plunge, leave eternity, and go into purgatory.

'That way you come back go to the Lord repented and go to heaven,' said Archangel Raphael.

The archangel disappeared over the clouds and I was alone in purgatory, having crossed the chasm into a vast desert with the sun beating down.

There was not a drinking well for miles and I was thirsty but I recalled what Jesus said: 'If you are thirsty I would give you water from eternal life.'

I repeated what Jesus said and before I took another step my thirst was gone.

What lies ahead is never-ending desert awaiting my fate.

Chapter 2

The Monastery

In the past life I was tempted by women, especially prostitutes. With remorse I entered the monastery praying forgiveness. My new name was Brother Andrew. I was called by the monks 'randy Andy'.

My previous wicked ways were absolved in my confession, like Mary Magdalene, a lady of the night and repented. She was the first one to see Jesus alive, risen from the dead.

I left the monastery because it is strict order, getting up at 4.30am and working all day and missing women. There was a freedom for an itinerant monk, wandering from town to town in what St. Benedict, the father of Western monasticism, referred to it as 'futile'. To me it was the freedom to go where I want and pray for the people I met, above all the fairer sex.

I walked for miles and came to the road which led me into a valley surrounded by palm trees. Beyond the palm trees there was a castle with high-walled and large mortar bricks. It was a fortress being guarded by two armed guards. I approached the castle and the guards stepped forward and questioned me about my journey and what I was doing there.

'I've come to bear witness to the Good News,' I said.

The guards opened the door. There was a long corridor inside the palace which led me into the lounge and the spacious bedroom. There on the bed was the Queen of harlots, Jezebel, with the scanty-dressed harlots serving her.

'Have you come to speak with me?' said Jezebel, a long black hair flowing to her waist. She had a bright red lipstick and a purple headscarf. 'Sit down and rest awhile. You've had a long journey. My servants will give you some wine and a massage,' she said, beckoning the harlots.

No sooner had she given the order, the harlots had me on my back massaging me and serving wine. One of the harlots, Scarlet, a young virgin, came forward and kissed me and fondled me until I was aroused.

'Now you go to Jezebel and she will oblige,' said the virgin, and bid her a hasty retreat. I took my pants to cover up my manhood, but there was Jezebel with her talons to strike, standing over me. 'Now you're aroused I will show you what you've been missing. Come to me, the Queen of harlots.'

'No, no,' I protested. 'I've come to repent. Let me go.'

'Repent?' exclaimed Jezebel. 'What's for? Making love is not a sin.'

'It is sin if you're not married,' I protested. 'The Lord said so.'

'You've met God?' said Jezebel, annoyed.

'I've met Him,' I said, 'and you the Queen of harlots will rot in hell unless you repent.'

'We've all sinned,' said Jezebel. 'Come here.' She invited me to sit beside her. 'Your arousal with the virgin harlot it's not a crime. It's exciting,' she said, caressing my manhood with her slender hands.

'I'm in purgatory to repent,' I protested. 'Let me go.'

Then Jezebel enticed me into feeling her enormous breasts. They were sensuous and made me want seduce her. She lifted her arched back, grasping me with tightly around my buttocks to tempt me.

'Come inside of me,' cooed Jezebel, 'that's not a sin.'

'It is and I'm not going to hell,' I retorted.

With that I fled the castle never to be seen again.

It was a temptation that I had overcome, but there was more to come in my quest for repentance and redemption.

Chapter 3

Leprosy

I hiked all day across the desert, not a human in sight. But then I saw a light from a distance. It was a monastery, unlike the one I joined on earth all that time ago. The monastery did not suit me then as it was a contemplative order but this monastery was a godsend for I had not eaten for a week.

I knocked on the door and an elderly monk poked his nose around the door and said: 'Go away.'

'But I've come to pray with you,' I pleaded.

'Go away,' the monk said. 'We are lepers.'

I was shocked. Can it be that the monastery was chosen by the devil, that all of the monks were infected with leprosy? I retreated along the path away from the monastery on hearing those words.

Then suddenly the archangel Raphael appeared and said: 'You must go back to the monastery and pray for the monks and heal them.'

The archangel then took off up into the clouds and I was left alone. How I would go about healing the monks, the divine gift, which archangel Raphael had entrusted to me? I prayed for courage and set out for the monastery.

On entering the monastery grounds, a monk sitting by a tree called out: 'You must not enter, for God's curse is upon the community.'

'Do not be afraid,' I said, kneeling beside him. 'I have to come to heal you.'

I placed on my hands upon his head and asked the Lord to heal him of leprosy. The monk trembled before me and I called out to the Holy Spirit to cure him from a deadly disease.

'Heal him in the name of Jesus!' I ordered. After a few minutes the monk suddenly stood up and turned to me. 'The leprosy is gone. God bless you, my friend. You are a healer come from God,' he cried.

'The archangel Raphael sent me to the monastery to heal the sick,' I replied. 'Are you better now?'

'Indeed I am, praised God,' said the monk, looking at his healed hands. 'You must go to the Spiritual Father and tell him what you have done.'

I went to the reception and rang the bell. After a few minutes the door opened, there was a frail old man with a walking stick, his features all shivered up with leprosy. 'Don't come near me. What it is you want? The monks are dying here,' said the Spiritual Father.

'I have come to cure the monks of leprosy,' I said. 'There is a monk in the garden. I prayed for him and he's as good as new.'

'You cured him?' he asked, astonished.

'I was given the divine gift of healing by the archangel Raphael,' I said. 'Let me pray for you.'

'If you're a healer then by all means pray for me a sinner?' said the Spiritual Father. 'I committed adultery all those years ago and God sent me to purgatory and the devil cursed with a disease.'

'Have faith,' I asked him. 'Hold out your hands.' With that I prayed, my hands over his head, asking God forgive him and rid of the disease. After a few minutes he was cured.

'Gone is my leprosy, you made me whole again. Praise the Lord,' said the Spiritual Father.

I left him in his cell praising God and went to the brothers healing them of leprosy, giving thanks to the Lord and the archangel Raphael of his divine gift. The Spiritual Father called me in his office and he thanked me again for curing him and the brothers of leprosy.

'There is a convent not far from here,' said the father. 'You go to the convent and pray for the sisters to get well,' he said, urgently.

'What's wrong with the nuns?' I asked.

'Have you heard of the village of Salem in the United States?' he asked. 'Many years ago there was curse of witchcraft and the nuns were involved. You can go and pray for them. The nuns were bewitched when I last visited them,' said the Spiritual Father.

'Where is the convent?' I asked.

'About a mile from yonder,' said the monk.

I set out for the convent, fearing the worst.

Have I brought another temptation on me?

Chapter 4

The Convent

I made my way to the convent, a grey building with barred windows. It seemed like a prison with its high walls and secured gate. As I walked through the entrance suddenly a voice shouted out: 'Turn back. We don't have males here.' It was a voice of a nun tendering the goats.

'I've come to pray for the nuns,' I said. 'The archangel Raphael sent me.'

The nun, on hearing the archangel had sent me, raced to the office of Mother Superior and told her. The Mother Superior came out, looked me up and down, and said coldly: 'Are you a tramp?'

'No,' I said, 'I've come to heal the nuns.'

'Are you a doctor?' said the Mother.

'I am a healer called by the Holy Spirit and sent by the archangel Raphael,' I said. 'I've come from the monastery. The monks are healed of leprosy. You can phone the monastery if you want?'

'Heaven be praised,' cried the Mother Superior. 'Come in.'

The Mother Superior led me to her office and said that American nuns were the daughters of mothers, who had been involved in witchcraft in Salem. The mothers were hanged. 'The nuns have been out of minds for the past five years. Heaven help us! We cannot bear purgatory any longer,' she cried out.

'Are all the nuns possessed?' I asked.

The Mother Superior nodded, tears were rolling down her cheeks.

'Where are the nuns now?'

'They are in the chapel'

As fast as I could I made my way to the chapel. There were seven nuns in a fit, wailing and shouting their arms above their heads, crying out: 'Have mercy on us, have mercy on us. Take us out of purgatory, we pray.'

I was shocked by the nuns. They were about to go into seizures. The demons had possessed their souls and take them to hell if I had not intervened. The Mother Superior called them to stop and step forward and form a circle. 'This man is sent to heal you. He has been sent by the archangel Raphael and he has the power to heal you.'

I stood before the nuns with a crucified cross in my right hand and called out: 'In the name of Jesus, heal the nuns. Come out you evil spirits and show yourself and be gone from this convent.'

Suddenly there was a sound of a rush of air and the demons were gone out of the nuns and fled from the chapel.

The nuns rushed forward to greet me cheering loudly and raising their arms singing, 'Alleluias, Alleluias'.

The Mother Superior exclaimed: 'Praise the Lord. You have restored the convent's sanity. God bless you. Heaven awaits you.'

'Heavens no,' I said. 'God has further trials ahead for me. Pray for me a sinner.'

All the contemplative nuns were gathered around me saying I was a prophet and they all wanted to come with me on a journey beyond the desert away from purgatory. I told them they have vowed to stay at the convent and what would Mother Superior say if they were deserting the convent?

I said farewell to the nuns and wished them God's blessings and their entrance to heaven.

Chapter 5

The Twins

I set out along the road that leads to the never-ending desert. My thoughts were about the deeds I had accomplished, which were nothing compared with heaven. Avoiding temptations such as the harlot Jezebel, healing the monks' leprosy and delivering the nuns from possession, all of these deeds would be merits for me to free of purgatory. Or so I thought.

God has other plans to test me - women and wine, my Achilles heel! Ever since becoming a monk I had been chaste, but now I was in purgatory temptation was all around. The other side of the desert a town called Hell.

On seeing a light at a far distance I walk towards it and about a mile I came upon were two sisters in hiding in the woods. They were frightened and looked dishevelled, clinging to each other out of fear.

'Why are you afraid,' I said, concerned.

'My father,' said one of the sisters. 'He was about to sell us to slavery. My mother protested and he strangled her.'

'My God,' I exclaimed. 'What are your names?' I asked.

'I'm Anna and this is Rachel. We are twins,' she said, sobbing.

'Don't cry,' I said, holding their hands, 'come with me and I will protest you from your wicked father.'

They both got up and we left to go in the direction of a street where there was a bazaar and women gypsies dancing with group of musicians. We sat at a table and I ordered a bottle of wine to cheer the sisters up. After a few drinks I asked both if they wanted to dance. They got up to dance until Rachel said she had enough exercise and wanted to sit down. We went and sat down with Rachel and before I knew it I had finished off the wine and ordered another bottle.

I poured them a drink and before the band sang their last song I drank the remaining bottle. I admire the twins, their golden hair and slender legs and felt an urge to pursue it further, getting to know them.

'There's a hotel nearby we can stay there if you want,' I said. It was a long time ago when I had a drink and the alcohol was affecting me. We made our way to the hotel and I ordered champagne and flowers so the twins were relaxed. I looked at them in their short skirts sipping champagne and I in my intoxicated state I offered them a 'threesome'.

'What's that?' asked the twins, naively.

'I'll show you,' I said. I promptly helped Rachel and Anna undress and lay on the bed, invitingly to take their virginity.

'We've never been with a man before,' said Anna. 'You saved us from slavery. We want you be the first man to take our virginity.'

With that Rachel laid there on the bed as I made love to her. But Anna was more willing, lifting her breasts and arched her back as I took her virginity. They lay on the bed exhausted, enjoying the first sexual encounter.

We sat and talk about what the twins will do next. My thoughts were about repenting for what I had done in seducing the girls. What manner of a monk would something like that? My chances in heaven were like snowball in hell.

The twins were well pleased losing their virginity and got dressed and said goodbye. 'We're going to the bazaar and met some men,' said Rachel. 'You've awaken our sexual fantasies,' said Anna, laughing.

The sisters were going to find men, parading themselves as prostitutes, I thought. Heaven forbid! Are the twins selling themselves unconsciously of the father's wish to be sex slaves? It's my fault for having seduced the twins!

I left the town distraught and went into the desert praying God would be merciful, a wretched sinner, fallen from grace.

Chapter 6

Last Judgement

The long and weary road that leads to hell was about to appear before me. I cried out to the Lord in the desert as I sat down exhausted. In an instant there was the archangel Raphael standing before me.

'Come, we're going to meet your Maker,' said St. Raphael.

'But I'm not ready,' I protested, 'for I have sinned and need of repentance.'

'What is your sin,' asked the Archangel.

'Temptations of the flesh,' I said, dejected. 'I have seduced two virgins.'

'We are all sinners,' said St. Raphael. 'Come, let us go.'

There was a rush of wind, ten times a force of a gale, and took the archangel and me up into the clouds to heaven, where the Lord sits in the Last Judgement.

I trembled before the Almighty God as I stood before Him. The scroll of my life was put before Him, like a video playback. On reading it He looked up, pointing his finger as if I deserved eternal damnation, saying:

'You called out to me in the desert repenting your sins, and now that you have made some merits in purgatory on healing the monks and nuns, you will enter heaven. Come, you are welcome into My Kingdom.'

Hearing that I fell before the Lord, saying: 'Thanks be to

God. You have saved me from eternal hell. I overcame purgatory and now I will see a heaven, a new earth, and eternal life.'

Chapter 7

Banquet

A Christian festival was taking place and the all the angels and archangels and seraphim and cherubim were present. The archangel Raphael greeted me with a kiss of peace and I followed him into the banquet.

There at the head of the table was the Lord Jesus with Mary, the mother of God, on his right and Joseph, her spouse, St. John the Baptist, the apostles, Peter and Paul, and St. Francis. All welcomed me to the table, the heavenly banquet Jesus had promised to all who believed.

Outside there were dancing girls and fireworks and all sorts of entertainments like you would see on earth. It was overwhelming. All of the Christians were clothed in white robes with golden belts and there were a chorus of angels singing Alleluias, Alleluias. It was pure bliss.

Then, to honour me, the Lord raised His glass and thanked me for the trials and tribulations in the past life and welcomed me into heaven. I lifted my glass and said thanks for saving me, a wretched sinner. I turned the Mary, the Mother of God, and asked her how she had lived through the trauma of her son dying on the cross.

'A sword pierced my heart,' said Mary, 'but then I knew about the resurrection before it happened. Jesus told me long before Mary Magdalene met Jesus in the garden after the resurrection.'

'When you were told?' I asked, inquisitively.

'When Jesus was coming into Jerusalem the last time. He told me that within three days of his death He would rise up. And so He did!' said Mary, beaming.

'Did you know he was the Son of God when he was born?' I asked, astounded.

'The archangel Gabriel told me before He was born,' said Mary.

'What did he say?' I asked.

'When I conceived by the Holy Spirit, Gabriel came to me. I was to give birth to Emmanuel, the Son of God, and I was to name is Jesus,' said Mary.

'What did Joseph say?' I asked, curiously.

'At first he called off the wedding because he said that I'd been unfaithful. But then he had the dream of me being conceived by the Holy Spirit then he forgave me and he married me.'

'A sacred blessing,' I said. 'Joseph did right.'

Joseph looked up at me and smiled.

I turned to the one I admired, the forerunner, St. John the Baptist, sitting beside me.

'Why are you called the forerunner?' I asked.

'I'm called that because I was the one who called out in the desert He's the One. Prepare the way of the Lord. Make his path straight. Every valley filled in and every mountain and hill to be laid low. Winding ways will be straightened and rough roads made smooth and all mankind shall see the salvation of God. This is the Lamb of God that he takes away the sins of the world. I'm not worthy to undo the sole of his sandal. This is why I'm called a forerunner.'

'Are you a prophet,' I asked.

'Yes, but in the past life,' said St. John the Baptist. 'Now we're in Heaven and I'm not prophesying. It's been done.'

Peter and Paul were sitting opposite as they agreed. 'I was martyred in Rome. The soldiers put me upside down to crucify me. If the Lord wasn't there I would have perished in the Colosseum,' said St. Peter.

'So with me,' agreed St. Paul, 'the Lord himself saved me.'

St. Francis was sipping his wine, looking up at St. John the Baptist said: 'My God, you did well.'

St. Francis, a 12th century saint, who founded the Franciscan order, was the first of many saints to have followed Jesus by renouncing the world and its material possessions. He lived an austere life and preached and fed the animals and begging from town to town.

Now in the 21 century it is a crime for begging.

'The world has gone mad,' said St. Francis, despondently. 'The prince of darkness is come.'

'For now,' interceded Jesus, 'but I will return on the Second Coming and banish the prince of darkness.'

'When are you returning?' I asked, hopefully.

'When God tells me,' answered Jesus. 'Now you must go and visit your relatives who are now enjoying eternal life.'

With that I bowed my head, and after saying goodbye to Mary, John the Baptist, St. Francis and the apostles, I took my leave and entered the realms of heaven.

Chapter 8

Wives

On entering heaven there was fragrance so sweet it reminded me of Christmas back on earth when I opened my presents. The room was full of joy.

In my white robe I visited my mother Olive in her palace, together my second wife Sarah, who lived nearby. They greeted with open arms.

'Where is my first wife Sherma?' I asked.

'She gone to Buddha-land,' said my mother. 'She will come to know Jesus in time. Come, we have refreshments in the garden.'

We all sat around the garden table and mother poured us tea and we talked about our time was earth. Sarah said while on earth she didn't meet the ex-wife. 'Why on earth not?' she asked.

'You weren't around then,' I remarked. 'You were not born.'

'That's unusual name, Sherma' remarked Sarah.

'Her uncle was driving a Sherman tank in the Second World War and when she was born her parents abbreviated her name to Sherma.'

'Where you did meet?' Sarah asked, pointedly.

'I met her in a bar in Montreal,' I recalled. 'Sherma was with a man named Hollywood Stan and they didn't have a spare room to consummate their affair. I offered them my flat. The next morning Stan was gone and I introduced myself and got to know her. She was a model, six feet tall and red hair with big blue eyes. She stayed in my flat and before long we were married in a few months. She was stunning but there was a flaw to her. She was addicted to prescription pills, barbiturates. In the end I called her doctor and complained if the pills were prescribed any more I would refer the doctor to the medical authorities. Having no barbiturates she went to the pharmacy stocked up with codeine tablets. She was on them for the eight years until finally I got divorced.'

'That was hell!' said Sarah.

'It was. We had rows but I turned to Christianity and started painting. We went to a church one time and she admired the Baptists but she never went back there. We had a few happy times together, but I was drinking and she told me take valiums, which I became addicted and withdrawal was worse than heroin. I was in hospital for a month, but she never came to visit me. Sherma was a white witch. It seemed to tie in with her being a Buddhist.'

'How did you cope in withdrawal?' Sarah asked.

'It was hell,' I said, 'Paranoia was unending. I walked from the hospital down to the river and thought about by jumping in and ending it all. It was hell and it never seems to go away.'

'All that is in the past now, you are in eternal life,' said mother, consoling. 'God forgives you,' said Sarah. 'Come and see my house and pool. You'll love it."

I said goodbye to my mother and I walked with Sarah along the path decorated with orange trees and palm trees before reaching a white house on the hill overlooking a lake. It was a magnificent house, two floors and a patio and a pool. She took me inside into the lounge and a spiral stairs to a bedroom.

'What do you think of my house?' asked Sarah

'It's huge' I said. 'Can I see the pool?'

We went outside to the back garden and there was a pool as big as the Olympics pool, the length of about 50 metres.

'Can I take a dip,' I asked, forgetting that I had no trunks. Sarah took off her underwear and we dived in naked as when we were first born. I watched as Sarah with her blonde hair as she gracefully swam the length of the pool. 'You try,' she said. We swam together, forgetting that we were naked.

I sat beside her next to the pool and I looked at her beautiful body, slender legs and golden hair that fell down to her waist. She was in her prime, her beauty was such to behold, so much younger than I first met her on earth. I reached out to gently kiss her on the mouth, being her husband she would respond.

'Couples do not marry in heaven,' said Sarah, she insisted. 'It's in the Bible.'

'Can't we make love?' I asked, disappointed, 'I've never seen you so beautiful.'

'You can love me and not make love for we are spiritual,' said Sarah. 'You have not forgotten that?'

'I love you and want you to have our baby,' I said, urgently.

'We are spirits, you understand! Sarah said, earnestly. 'We are not maternal beings like before on earth. We have free spirits and don't reproduce. It is going back to earth and having babies. It is a never ending cycle from being born and dying until suffering comes to an end in eternity.'

'You sound if you're a Buddhist,' I said. 'Are you in to reincarnation?'

'No, I'm not,' said Sarah, emphatically. 'Life begins at

conception and through suffering we become purified and take our place in heaven, don't you see? There is no reincarnation, we are in eternity.'

I learned over and kissed her cheek. 'Thanks, my little philosopher.'

Sarah took me to lounge and offered me a drink. 'It's heavenly champagne,' she said, raising her glass.

'What about the Moslems? I said, 'where are they going?'

'They will be heaven later,' Sarah said, 'when they turn to Christ. The Jews are the same.'

'Islam is created out of false ideology,' I said. 'It is a false religion. Muslims are turning away from Our Lord. That's why some Muslims terrorists are killing people in the name of Allah.'

'All will be well in the end,' Sarah said. 'Eventually all must turn to Christ and be saved.'

'What if the person doesn't?'

'It up to the Lord,' said Sarah.

'But the Bible states that all people rejecting Christ will perish, no heavenly dwelling, but eternal damnation,' I said.

'We'll see,' said Sarah. 'You don't mention your dad? Where is he now?'

'He's not in heaven,' I said, sadly 'He believes in reincarnation and wants to come back as a cat. Those were his words.'

Sarah held my hands and hugged me. 'You poor dear,' she said, 'now we must go upstairs and I'll show my art work.' We climbed the spiral staircase and entered a large room and there was a small art studio and canvases and easel in the corner. A large painting of Madonna and Child were on the easel.

'How long have you been working on that?' I asked, studying

the canvas and touching the paint.

'Don't touch!' said Sarah. 'It's not dry yet. I have been working on it for a couple of months now. Have you seen Mary? Is the portrait like her?'

'Remarkable. I talked with her yesterday and it is identical. You're a true artist. Have you painted our Lord?'

'He's coming to sit for me next week,' said Sarah, delighted. 'Then I shall be a true artist, I hope.'

Chapter 9

The Gathering

The archangels, the cherub and seraphic and all the angels were gathering together in the Golden Cathedral to hear the Lord sermon on the kingdom. The crowd followed them into the cathedral and waited for Him to appear. Sarah and I were waiting with deep breathes as the Lord appeared high up on the balcony to address us.

'My brothers and sisters, you will have witnessed in many rooms in my Father's house joy and everlasting peace. You had travelled the earthly life with many trials and tribulation and you have all come through. Welcome to my kingdom. Peace upon you,' said the Lord.

'You will no doubt have many questions about what happened to the past on earth with all the upheavals and pestilence, genocide and wars. It's gone with Lucifer, the prince of darkness. You are living in eternity but you will recall your life on earth, the good and the bad, now that you will be living in peace. Blessings be upon you.'

On returning home I told Sarah that I too recalled the sins that I had done as well as the good deeds on earth.

'What sins are they?' asked Sarah, accusingly.

'I was a philanderer,' I confessed.

'You were married before,' she said, disapprovingly. 'What were the other sins?'

'Well, before I was called me a ladies' man,' I recalled. 'But I don't want to dig up earthly past. We are in heaven.'

Sarah, as all women do, insisted on telling her. 'The Lord says we are recalled our good and bad days. What are the bad days?'

'Will you see my house on the lake?' changing the subject. 'It's not as grand as yours, but it's spacious and nice.'

Sarah frowned. 'I want to see but tell me before I go.'

'All right,' I said, unravelling my brain as to what sexual sins I had committed.

'I had affairs as the teenager, as we all do, but I fell in love with Donna.'

'How old was she?' insisted Sarah.

'She was fifteen,' I confessed.

'She's a child!' admonished Sarah.

'Not with sex,' I insisted. 'She led me into her bedroom and discovered she was a Scorpio and sex mad. Girls mature differently nowadays, they even get married younger. In the middle ages girls marry at the age of twelve.'

'We aren't living in the middle ages,' said Sarah. 'Shame on you!' With that she threw her nose in the air and stormed off.

Sarah is forgetting that all those sins I committed on earth are absolved now that we are in heaven.

Chapter 10

Madonna

I was summoned by the archangel Michael who defeated Satin in heaven to explain why I was attracted so many girls in earth and why I was infatuated with them now.

'It is in our genes to procreate and have children,' I said, matter-of-factly.

St. Michael spread his wings and confronted me: 'You are in heaven now. We are like angels. There is no more sex. You must renounce all your thoughts about sex, if you don't you will be cast down to hell. There's no way back.'

The thought of hell terrified me and having gone through purgatory. 'I was attracted to girls in the past, not now,' I said, pleading. 'There is no romance. We are like brother and sisters, we're family.'

'Well said,' remarked archangel Michael. 'On earth you had a father and mother but in heaven you have the spiritual father, Our Lord, and the mother of God.'

'Sometimes I feel romantic to my wife,' I confessed, 'knowing that in heaven we don't have wives, as you said.'

Archangel Michael lowered his wings. 'That's right,' he said. 'We shall meet again,' then like a bird he flew up into the clouds and he was gone.

I pondered over his words and thought about the many affairs, and like Our Lord said, we can look back on our earthly lives and I don't regret it. If I saw Donna in heaven she would be the same adorable girl, if not more so when I sex with her, the same golden hair and beautiful breasts, urging me on to seduce her.

I went out to the lake and there was a huge waterfall surrounded by orange and lemon trees and rows of lilies as far as the eye could see. Beside the lake people were sitting and talking how they've come be there in paradise.

I glanced at them and there was Donna in a pink bathing suit and golden hair lying in the sun. She saw me and jumped to her feet and threw her arms around me as though it was for the first time.

'My God, where have you been? Donna asked, excitedly. 'How come you are in heaven?'

'I don't know,' I said, awkwardly. 'Mercy of God, I guess.'

'Do you remember what we got up to our past life?' Donna said, coyly.

I looked at her fine figure with golden locks and ample breasts. 'You look so divine, more beautiful than I first saw you all those years ago on earth.'

'You were horny then,' Donna said, teasing. 'It's all in the past. I have turned over a new leaf. Did you know I've become a virgin again?'

'Don't say,' I said gobsmacked.

'Yes, on entering heaven I became a virgin,' she said. 'It's a wonderful gift, don't you think?'

I looked into her blue crystal eyes and I could see a new creature, a heavenly soul so pure I could see God in those eyes. 'It's amazing, a new person. You are like an angel.'

'We're so blessed,' said Donna.

'I see now that you were called Donna,' I said, laughing, 'it goes with Madonna.'

'She was a virgin when she gave birth to Jesus,' she said, 'that's why I'm called Donna.'

We went for a walk beside the lake, a gentle breeze parted her golden hair, her smile was angelic and we walked hand in hand.

'Have you had a child?' I asked, curiously.

'No,' said Donna happily. 'Now I'm born again for Jesus and like Madonna, I'm a virgin.'

'But you missed in the earthly love life, surely?' I asked, curiously.

'Sometimes' said Donna.

'You missed making love?' I asked, looking at her breasts.

'Occasionally,' she said, doing up her bra straps. 'But we are in heaven and we don't wish to be reminded.'

I thought about the numerous times we had sex in the past life and the countless times we had skinny dipping in the sea.

'Do you want to make love?' I asked, hesitatingly.

Donna hugs me, putting her golden locks on my shoulder, and said coquettishly: 'I want to, but now I'm a virgin.'

All the temptations of the flesh became rushing back as I caressed her beautiful breasts and took her hand and placed it on my manhood.

'My God, you're bigger than before,' said Donna, surprised.

'Your breasts are enormous,' I said, feeling them. I took off her knickers and was about to take her virginity when I heard a voice cry out: 'Stop!'

It was the archangel Michael. 'Don't touch her,' he warned, his wings outstretched, admonishing me.

'I was about to make love. Is that a sin, making love?' I asked.

'I told you sex is an earthly pleasure. Go ahead, you will fall from heavenly grace and from there you go to purgatory or even hell. It's the way of the human soul, to go up and go down. You have the chosen to go down into purgatory where the soul will suffer all because of your sin,' said the archangel.

'Love is all that matters,' I said, matter-of-factly.

'You so-called love is lust and you will devour her and send the pair of you to purgatory. There is no sex in heaven. It's pure and you will be cast out.

'But I love her,' I said, lamenting over his words.

With that the archangel unfolded his wings and like a darting arrow flew up in the clouds.

I looked at Donna apprehensively.

'I told you so,' she said, smugly and walked away.

Chapter 11

New Jerusalem

Nestled among the palm trees high above the Mediterranean Sea lays the New Jerusalem, the heavenly city to last through all eternity. The majestic gold temple reaching as far as the eye could see was the entrance to precinct where the 24 divine elders were seated in rows of rainbow coloured chairs. Above was the high altar was seated Our Lord, Jesus Christ.

The Pearly Gates were flung wide open to welcome the heavenly Christians gathered around the temple, bowing before His throne and worshipping with angels singing: 'Holy, Holy, Holy is the Lord Almighty.'

Inside the temple, robed in white with a golden belts and golden crowns, were the seraphim and cherubim and archangels praising Jesus, gazing at his holy face, the Lamb of God, where peace and love flowed.

A simple meal of oranges, grapes and figs were prepared before the 24 elders to sit in judgement before the earth was destroyed and the new earth was born.

The divine prosecutor addressed the elders saying that when the earth will be destroyed it will be the prince of darkness, the satanic monster Satan takes over. 'Sin covers the whole world, but those who believe in Christ are saved.'

An elder intervened and said that few would be saved. 'As

scripture says, few are saved because straight in the path of salvation.'

'That is so,' says the Lord 'We must pray for the souls who will go through tribulation. It is time for Rapture.'

The elders were astounded by the Rapture so soon. 'What caused it?' the elders asked Our Lord.

'The earth is plagued with climate change, pollution, sexual immorality and pride. But it's not that caused it. It's the sun!' said Our Lord.

'The sun is expanding, like all stars nearing the end, and its solar flares will burn up the earth and its solar system. The people have little time.'

'How long?' the elders asked.

'The Rapture is now,' said the Lord.

Chapter 12

Rapture

Christians in the temple prayed for relatives, who were in the midst of the Rapture, knowing that the earth will catch fire. Archangels said they were about to start a vigil for those who have been left behind on earth.

I fled to the mountain, the solitary place for pray, and found a cave away from the crowd. I was trained for the hermit in the monastery, praying for the end of the world to come.

Thank God I was in heaven far from the maddening crowd, who were caught up in the Rapture. Who will be saved? As scripture says all be saved who believe in Christ, but narrow is the gate. All of a sudden the archangel Raphael appeared.

'It is written,' said archangel Raphael, 'all that believe in their hearts that Christ is the son of God will be saved. The Rapture will be the separating the wheat from the chaff, sheep from the goats, believers separated from non-believers, and the Christian souls will go through the fire and come out purified, like the angels.'

'We shall see them in heaven?' I asked.

'Yes, they will come from the earth with pure hearts,' said St. Raphael.

'What about the rest?' I asked.

'In heaven, as you know, there are three sphere, one is the throne of the Almighty, Our Lord Jesus Christ, the second is the seraphim and cherubim, archangels and angels, and the third is divine elders and pure souls. In hell there are the same three spheres: One is the throne of Satan, the second is devils and demons and the third is the fallen souls.'

'Will they stay in hell forever?' I asked.

'It is as you say,' said the archangel. 'The demons will torment them and they will suffer eternally. Have you read about the damned will suffer eternally in Dante's Inferno? Pray for the souls going through Rapture. '

'Can we see the Rapture now?' I asked.

'You can see it on the big wide screen in New Jerusalem,' said St. Raphael, 'It's on now, thousands of people attending.'

With that he unfolded his wings and took off like a thunder bolt into the clouds.

I went to New Jerusalem and there was a mass of people crowding into a wide open screen for the Rapture live via satellite. The archangels and seraph and cherub and all the angels were there to witness the end of the world.

I looked at the sun looming in the far side of the screen approaching the earth with its 200 mile sun flares radiated so close to the earth. I heard people screaming from one end of the horizon to the other, burning with intense heat as the Rapture was about to happen.

I looked in the Bible to see what prophecy St John in Revelation would be their fate for the end of the world. The number of people that were Christians would be saved - only 144,000 souls! On reading closer, it found that of the 144,000 souls saved would be descends of the 12 tribes of Israel, namely the Christian souls who had converted down through the ages.

As I looked up at the screen billions of humans were being burnt alive as the earth disintegrated before our very eyes. The souls that were saved by Rapture into heaven were greeted by angels to meet Our Lord.

The remnants of the earth were burnt up by the sun, devouring all human life as the sun flares swept through the cosmos. Earth was finally obliterated.

Our Lord met the souls who had escaped but leaving their mortal bodies behind to perish in the fire. But on entering heaven they were given a new body, a spiritual body, which reigned for eternity.

The Christian souls had to go through Judgement Day and come out of the Rapture their hearts purified. The legions of angels dressed the people in white robes before meeting Our Lord.

All souls were damned for not believing in Christ, entered the third sphere of hell, an everlasting punishment for unrepentant sins.

On screen millions of people were being whip-lashed, beaten with iron bars and thousands were being executed, a second death of the soul. Such was the torments of hell.

In heaven, Our Lord received the Christians with their spiritual bodies robed with white silk and golden belts. Each one of them received a holy kiss from the Lord, who welcomed to his palace for a banquet, promised by scriptures as a reward for heaven.

Seated at the table was Tsar Nicholas of Russia and Tsarina Alexander, along with their five daughters and a son, film actress Marilyn Monroe, Elvis Presley, the King of Rock n' Roll, and the former president John Kennedy and Jacqueline Kennedy. They were welcome by the angels who surrounded them with praise.

All of those martyred were reminiscing about how they came to heaven, going back to the times the Russian revolution and how the Tsar and his family were executed and when the president John Kennedy was shot. The troubled Marilyn overdosed at 36 and Elvis died at 42, all 'shook up'.

I took the trouble during the banquet to ask Marilyn how she died. "It was a mistake. I overdosed on barbiturates,' said Marilyn. 'Now that I'm in paradise, wow, I've been blessed.'

'You were a great actress,' I remarked. 'But you were a sex symbol and men were ogling you, even your boobs.'

'Wow, it was something,' said Marilyn, laughing. 'There were downsides to it, even the president stood me up.' She looked across at the banqueting table and said in that inimitable way: 'Wow, he's here.'

Elvis intervened and said he was singing at the Pearly Gates bar that evening and if we would be welcome to come along. I looked at Marilyn and we off to the bar hearing Elvis singing 'Love Me Tender.'

I held Marilyn's hand and we kissed in a friendly way. After we left I took her to the house and she asked to come in with for a drink.

'Not tonight Marilyn,' I said, 'I've got to pray for souls in Rapture'.

'Ah gee,' she said, and tenderly kissed me goodnight.

Chapter 13

The Lovers

The morning was eternally blissful as the sun swept over the valleys and into the city, New Jerusalem. I set off to see my wife Sarah. She was about to paint a portrait of Jesus coming over to sit in the afternoon. It was a major blessing to paint Our Lord in all his glory.

On earth Michelangelo would not have dreamed of painting the Lord to sit for him, let alone Leonardo de Vinci or that matter Matisse, who painted the chapel in the south of France before his death.

When I got there Sarah had a message from Our Lord saying he will postpone it for another day because he is to welcome the people who have escaped the Rapture.

'I'm disappointed but the Christians are being blessed into heaven,' said Sarah, folding her hands in praise.

'Our Lord will come soon for a portrait, I'm sure,' I said, hopefully.

Sarah looked dismayed, pointing to the easel. 'I'm not certain. Our Lord has many duties to perform, far more than He did on earth.'

'You can paint me if you like?' I volunteered.

'That's nice of you,' said Sarah. 'But I can't paint if He's not coming, you understand,' putting the easel back and paint brushes away.

I held out my hand to console her but she turned and hugged me. I felt her warm embrace and then suddenly she kissed me, her lips were soft and tender, as though we had first met. I put my arms around to feel her embrace and then the doorbell rang.

It was Donna.

'I followed you,' said Donna. 'I thought you would come here.'

'I know all about you,' said Sarah, fuming. 'You seduced my husband.'

'Andy seduced me,' retorted Donna.

I intervened and told the women the affair was a thing of the past, but now me are in heaven they would be friends and make up. They looked at each other, smiled and kissed on the cheek.

'It's nice to meet you,' said Donna, waltzing in like a prima donna. She flounced her skirt as she sat down and adjusted her bra. 'I like the furniture and the colours of the walls. Hey, do I see an easel in the corner. Do you paint Sarah?'

'Yes, but not today,' she said. 'I don't have a sitter. Our Lord was coming today but he's very busy and postponed it.'

'The Lord postponed?' said Donna, aghast. 'I will sit for you?' said Donna, volunteering. 'I can be a life model, if you want?'

Sarah looked at Donna, her blonde hair and beautiful smile, and turned me and said: 'If you don't mind, I would like a word with Donna in private.'

'Suit yourself,' I replied, 'if you don't won't to paint me. Donna has an amazing figure, you'll see.' With that I left the women alone to gossip.

Donna disrobed and sat on the couch. Sarah studied her from a distance, her breasts were larger and her curves were rounded like a model.

'My, you look like a glamour model with a figure like yours. Have you had many lovers on earth, apart from my husband?'

'I was promiscuous,' said Donna, confessing. 'I was bisexual, but that's all gone now. We are immortal.'

'Are you sure?' asked Sarah.

'Immortal?'

'No, you're past sex life,' Sarah said. 'You don't get horny?'

'Sometimes,' remarked Donna, staring down at her cleavage. 'Do you like my boobs?'

'They're lovely.'

'Do you find them sexy?' asked Donna.

'A little,' said Sarah, focussing on her painting.

'Andy does, he tried to seduce me last week,' said Donna, matter-of-factly.

'That's Andy for you,' said Sarah. 'Now keep your head still.'

Sarah went over to the Donna adjusting her pose, pointing her head in the direction of the canvas. Donna without a further ado turned her face towards her and kissed passionately on her lips.

Sarah, overcome by the surprised kiss, yielded to the temptation and melted in her arms, kissing her gently back.

That evening the women slept together.

Chapter 14

Spiritual Love

The sun turned to bright yellow as I walked through the city to meet Sarah a few days after I left in a huff. She was sitting in the garden admiring the view when I walk down the path.

'It's a breathtaking view,' I said, taking in the mountains far away. Changing the subject I turned to Sarah: 'Did you paint Donna?' I asked.

'You want to see it?' Sarah said, smiling. She led me into the studio and in the corner was a reclining nude of Donna.

'Wow,' I said. 'She has amazing body.'

'That's kind of you to say that,' said Donna, appearing from the bedroom.

'I take it Our Lord never came to sit for his portrait? I said, turning to Sarah.

'He'll come another day,' said Sarah. 'He's too busy right now.'

'And you painted Donna instead – in the nude!' I said, in a hint of jealousy.

'I like being nude,' remarked Donna, revealing her figure.

'Aren't you forgetting something, you too Sarah?' I said, remonstrating. There are repercussions for lesbians.'

'Like the kettle calling the pot black,' said Sarah. 'Come on, you have the urge now and again.'

'That so!' called out Donna. 'You tried to seduce me but your archangel told you to stop it.'

'I repented,' I said. 'Have you any idea what happens if you two make love?'

'That's what Our Lord teaches – love!' said Donna, romantically.

'You mix love with passion,' I said, indignantly. 'Love is spiritual - not flesh.'

'You can talk!' said Sarah, 'randy Andy.'

'Don't call me that,' I said, 'you are in heaven. A pure heart wouldn't say such a thing.'

'I'm sorry,' said Sarah, 'I'm impatient, lately.'

'No wonder you're frustrated,' I said. 'The Lord didn't come for his portrait.'

'What repercussions are they?' asked Donna. 'We only slept together.'

Sarah blushed. 'It was only once, but it won't happen again, will it Donna?'

'Maybe,' she said, smiling.

'Repercussion is to leave heaven and not come back,' I said, protesting. 'That is the price of sin.'

'God is merciful,' said Sarah.

There was a knock on the door and Sarah went to see who it was. I went over to the canvas and studied the subject and colour of painting. 'It is a great painting,' I said.

'It's a reclining nude' said Donna. 'It's why you like it!'

Sarah came back into the room and introduced no other than Our Lord. He entered the room with a sign of peace and love. 'Now you want to paint a portrait of me? Where do I sit?

Sarah told him to sit in the chair and Donna hurriedly to

get his drink. Sarah asked Our Lord to look out of the window. 'That way I can paint a profile of you,' said Sarah.

With delicate brushwork she was able to paint Our Lord with hues of gold and red and finishing it off with a halo in next to no time.

Sarah turned to Jesus and said the painting was finished. She beckoned him to see the portrait.

'Now that divine,' said Our Lord, 'you have managed to capture me.'

Sarah and Donna hugged each other in delight.

'Now you have two sisters to look after you,' said the Lord, turning to me.

'There not sisters, but two lovers,' I blurted out.

Sarah was livid and scorned me in front of Our Lord. 'You shouldn't be saying that, you scoundrel.'

'That's fact,' I said. 'You can't hide anything from Our Lord.'

Sarah went to Jesus and got on her knees and pleaded: 'It was only once I fell from grace. Be merciful to me and forgive me.'

The Lord stood up and held her in his arms saying: 'I forgive you. Be in love and not sin.' Turning to the portrait, he stood back and admired it. 'It is a wonderful painting.'

Donna threw herself at Jesus feet and sobbed. 'I too am I'm need of forgiveness.' Jesus held her hand and forgave her.

'I have to go and meet with the archangels,' said Jesus. 'We have the Olympics Games in the New Jerusalem stadium soon.'

'The Olympics Games,' I repeated, dumbfounded. 'It's absolutely great you should have the Olympics in heaven. It's wonderful. Can I compete?'

Jesus declared: 'All of you will compete. You're in heaven.'

Chapter 15

Olympics Games

The Olympics Games at the New Jerusalem Stadium were opened by Our Lord. The Games would last a month, giving the large number athletes time to compete. The opening ceremony was heralded angels blowing bugles and athletes waving to the crowds as they paraded around the stadium.

It was like the Olympics on earth, but it was more magnificent as the first games were in heaven. The athletes were competing in the eternal spirit of the games. For the first event was for 100 metres.

The field events were my speciality, namely the pole vault and the javelin. The higher I could get and the distance I could throw would get me higher into heaven, despite my shortcomings. So I believed.

Sarah was in the crowd urging me on as I managed to pole vault at my first attempt at 20ft, breaking my own record on earth, 19ft. In the 1500 metres I was last but managed to get second with one lap to go. A sprint finish down the straight and I won with a delighted crowd behind me.

I ran over to Sarah and she gave me a hug and a lingering kiss, which invited me for intimate romance, despite our heavenly relationship was platonic.

In heaven our hearts as pure as the driven snows, yet what a lingering kiss does to well-endowed athlete. I embrace her and then I went on lap of honour to celebrate my win.

Archangel Michael presented me with a Gold Medal for having won the 1500 metres, although he warned not to get intimate with Sarah.

Donna and Sarah were in the 800 metre final up against the woman, Eva, who won the year before on earth. On the first lap Sarah was in the lead but on the back straight Eva was edging into the lead. On the final lap Sarah and Eva were overtaken by outstanding Donna who raced away to win.

There was tumultuous roar from the crowd as Donna gave a lap of honour for she broke the record by five seconds. I dashed over and embraced her, not knowing if she respond, but she hugged me and thanked me for my support.

Sarah and Donna headed off to the pool to relax and I, forgetting the archangel warning, went with them in the same unisex changing rooms. Sarah changed into a pink costume and Donna - she had no inhibitions - was in her birthday suit, her beautiful breasts and curvaceous figure flaunted past me.

Several men watched her as she dived into the pool. Sex is alive even in heaven, so I thought. I followed Sarah into the pool as we caught up with Donna swimming the backstroke.

'The guys are eyeing you up,' I said to Donna, as she glided to the pool edge. 'Your boobs' turns them on.'

'What turns you on?' Donna asked, raising her eyebrows.

'You running the 800 metres in record time,' I said, jokingly.

Sarah looked at Donna with beady eyes. 'You've egged the lads on already. Don't you know that we're in heaven?'

'I know what men like,' Donna replied, raising her arms above her head.

'Your enormous breasts,' I said, laughing.

We left the stadium and we walked back to Sarah's house as the sun sets below the mountains. We were tired after the sports day and after a meal we got into Sarah's bed, all three of us snuggled together.

'We are in sisters and brothers,' Sarah said, cuddling up with me on the right side and Donna on the left. 'We're family.'

'Don't think so,' said Donna, feeling my manhood under the sheets.

'Stop it, Donna,' I said, taking her hand away. 'Don't you realise what beauty there is all around. Beauty is eternal.'

'Your willy is,' said Donna, rubbing against me.

'We are in heaven and there's no sex,' admonished Sarah. 'We are all God's children and we're in eternity. There's no more nookie.'

'Why not?' said Donna, 'Andy got the urge.'

'No, I've not got the urge,' I said, getting out of bed. 'There's no more hanky-panky.'

'No-one told me that before I came to heaven,' said Donna, disappointedly.

'There's no reproduction in heaven, silly,' said Sarah. 'You've got hang-ups from your earthly affairs.'

'Look who's talking,' said Donna. 'You had me in bed the other night.'

'It wasn't sex,' insisted Sarah, 'it was love making.'

'You could have fooled me,' Donna sneered. 'How come we don't produce babies? Are we infertile?'

'We don't produce babies because we are in heaven,' I said. 'Babies are born in the material world but the earth is no more, obliterated by the sun. That's why we don't reproduce because we are eternal,'

'I don't get it,' fumed Donna. 'We have the same earthly bodies. Why can't we make love?'

'We are not the same, we have spiritual bodies,' I said. 'Why can't you understand? Do you want to leave heaven and go to another material planet, just like earth, and have babies? You are going back to the cycle of birth and death and suffering. Do you want that?"

'I'm confused,' Donna said. 'I want to have children. It's in my DNA.'

'I must confess you have a beautiful body,' I said, 'but you're worldly, not of the spirit.'

'Thanks, but you're lusting after my body all the same,' said Donna. 'Men are all the same.'

Chapter 16

Divine Crusaders

I was summoned to Sphere One, the highest gate in heaven, to attend the meeting of Our Lord and the archangels. Archangel Michael addressed the synod, but not my sins for I had confessed them already.

For this was a matter of urgency. Heaven was being infiltrated by a group of demons, who disguised themselves as Christians. Their aim was to usurp the kingdom and sit Saturn on his throne.

'Our aim is to defeat them before they get any further,' announced archangel Michael. 'I will appoint Divine Crusaders. I'm appointing you as deputy to destroy them in battle.'

'There is no battle in heaven, only peace,' I protested.

'I have sent angels as far the outward heaven. The demons are about to enter side gate,' said archangel Michael. 'The Divine Crusaders will cast them out and send to hell.'

Our Lord stood up and prayed for Holy Spirit to win. 'I will defeat Saturn and my blessings upon you and the Divine Crusaders. Go forth.'

St. Michael recruited twelve angels who vowed their allegiance to the Divine Crusaders. With the Holy Spirit we journey to the far corner of the heaven to await the demons about to infiltrate heaven.

In the distance I could see the demons scaling the wall

wearing white robes Christians wore to enter heaven.

St. Michael and I stood at the top wall with the angels and he warned them not to enter heaven or else they would surrender to the Holy Ghost. Their leader, Lucifer, came forth and wielded his sword and the demons spitting fire.

They advanced near the top of the wall and about to enter heaven when the Divine Crusaders stood firm and held out the Cross and prayed for the Holy Spirit to banish them.

At this Lucifer and the demons were blindfolded by the Holy Spirit and fell down in to the pit of everlasting hell.

St Michael prayed that Heaven was restored. 'Blessings upon you and the Divine Crusaders. My congratulations for an epic win. You will each receive a gold medal for your achievements and a parade in Heavenly Boulevard.'

The Divine Crusaders and I as deputy returned to New Jerusalem with a fanfare and loud cheering by the thousands of people lined the boulevard. We were presented to Our Lord by the archangel Michael and announced the Divine Crusaders saved them from Lucifer and the demons attempting to infiltrate the heaven by posing as Christians.

'They even cursed and spat fire on the Divine Crusaders from all sides as they attempted to climb the heavenly walls, but the Divine Crusades rained down upon them the Holy Spirit and cast them down into the pit of destruction,' cried out St. Michael.

I stood before the Lord as He presented a gold medal and each one of the Divine Crusaders. He praised them for the courage and divine faith and declared a month of celebration on their heroic battle.

St. Michael took me aside and said thank you for being his

deputy and my courage and diligence. He would promote me as the Protocol of the Outer Heavenly district, which demons had fought for our kingdom.

Chapter 17

Salome

The Outer Heavenly region was vast. I made a map of the area and taking provisions for the journey and my sword, in case there was trouble in the district, for the demons had already attempted to usurp the kingdom.

It took me a week to find a place where I was staying, the outskirts of the barren land, a far cry from New Jerusalem. I walked along the path leading to my new home. As I entered I was greeted by a nun wearing a white veil and gold habit. Her name was Salome, the nurse, whose duty was to look after me and tend my needs.

Salome led me into the lounge and after I had a drink I took out a map of the district and surrounding areas. The map showed me that the Outer Heavenly region was in fact was a vast expanse of deserts an endless barren landscape.

'Why on earth did you come here?' I asked the nurse. 'It is barren.'

'I came here for you,' said Salome, 'I'm at your service.'

'How did you know I was coming?' I asked.

'A guardian angel told me,' she said, smiling. 'What are your duties here?'

'I'm sent here to watch out for any demons to might try and enter heaven,' I said, earnestly. 'I was promoted Protocol for this region. The demons last week tried to enter by force.'

'I heard about that,' said Salome, 'and the Divine Crusaders. You should take some rest now that you've had a long journey. I'll go and prepare your food and make up the bed.'

She bowed and departed with an endearing smile. I looked at the map and studied the terrain and where I should put the Divine Crusaders, the holy angels, on watch.

Salome brought the food in and disappeared to the bedroom. She made up the bed and brought out candles and ointments to indulge me in a massage. I was tired and my body needed to relax after a gruelling journey.

I disrobed and Salome had the ointment ready. She rubbed the ointment into my muscles with a soft motion, slowly soothing the aches all over my body.

'There now,' said Salome. 'You relax now and I'll give you a head massage.' As she soothes my head I look into her clear blue eyes and radiant smile as if I had seen her face before.

Then it dawned on me: she was one of those nuns of the convent I saw in Purgatory!

'Haven't I seen you before?' I asked. 'Were you in the convent when I healed the nuns?'

'You haven't forgotten me then,' said Salome. 'You saved my life and why I'm indebted to you and want to serve you.'

'It seemed ages ago you were in the convert. Age has not caught up with you. You look beautiful. What happened to the rest of the nuns?' I asked.

'They are in the convent, near New Jerusalem,' said Salome. 'They pray to Our Lord and you too for having saved their lives.'

'Bye God!' I said. 'You're a new nun.'

Salome leaned over me and kissed me on a cheek, a heart-felt embrace that was so warming I could not respond. I held her in my arms and kissed her tenderly and stroked her golden hair. She lay in my arms and I wondered if God has sent me a soul-mate, a friend, to share in heaven?

Salome turned to me and whispered in my ear that goes against what St. Michael taught me.

'I love you,' she said, earnestly.

'But an affair with a woman is against rules of heaven,' I said, indigently. 'St. Michael said so.'

'St. Michael does not like women,' said Salome, calmly. 'You should talk to archangel Raphael. He loves women and Our Lord too. Heaven allows you to make love.'

'That's so!?' I said, flabbergasted. 'But humans don't reproduce in heaven, so what is the point of making love? We are spiritual.'

'It bonds us together. If we make love, the two are one in body,' she said. 'We share the same fate, ever since Adam and Eve.'

'You want us to get married?' I suggested.

'If you want to,' said Salome, taking my hand.

'But there is no marriages in heaven, Our Lord said that,' I protested.

'All the same, we shall be in union, one body,' she said, with conviction.

I looked at Salome, her figure was voluptuous and breasts were perfect, like a divine virgin. It took a saint not make love to her. I reached out and kissed her on the lips and then a sudden conviction took hold of me. If I was to make love and the two became one body what would the archangel Michael say? Fornicating in heaven! I turned away, all confused.

'I'll talk to archangel Raphael,' I said, hesitatingly. 'He knows best. I'm going away for a few days to appoint the Crusaders.'

'I'll be waiting for you,' she said, kissing me goodbye. 'I love you.'

I waved goodbye to Salome, uncertain of her purity. She wants to be seduced. Could it be that the nuns I healed in the convent from witchcraft, passed down by mothers all those years ago in Salem, had come back and bewitched Salome?

Could it be witchcraft had infected her again turned into a nymphomaniac? Who could ever imagine that witchcraft, with its black magic, curses and hexes, could enter into heaven?

It was a sacrilege.

Chapter 18

Secret Affair

I set out for the mountain region where there was an angel guarding the flock of sheep in the valley, as King David did as a shepherds boy in Judah.

I rounded up the Divine Crusaders to defeat the demons if they entered heaven. We would arrange to meet on a side of a blue lake, a vast expanse leading to a side gate the demons attempted to enter before.

As a leader appointed to watch out for intrusions by the demons I was concerned for any signs of witchcraft, which I had healed the seven nuns in the convent in purgatory.

'Are the witches invading heaven?' asked John, a Crusader, concerned.

'Not to my knowledge,' I said, remembering what Salome had said about witchcraft in the convent.

'Do you think the demons will attack as before in the side gate?' asked John.

'There are many side gates,' I said, 'we must watch out for them. Vigilance is the key. Be ready with the Holy Spirit.'

Another of the crusaders stood up and said he had seen a sign of witchcraft before he came to the meeting.

'What sign did you see?' I asked, pointedly.

'My servant in my palace came into the bedroom and wanted to seduce me,' the crusader said. 'It is against the rules.'

'I will look into it,' I said. 'I too have met a similar fate.'

'When does the first crusader watch?' asked John.

'Right now,' I said, and sent a crusader to the side gate.

I questioned the crusader's account of witchcraft. Was the crusader's servant a nun in the convent? That's so then the nuns are re-infected in heaven again! A witch hunt was about to begin!

I called upon the archangel Raphael to intercede. But there was no answer from the archangel. I called John and he told me that all the archangels were about to honour Our Lord. As soldiers of Christ we are responsible for the security of heaven.

'When will the Archangel Raphael come back?' I asked, urgently.

'God knows,' said John.

I sent John to sort out the Divine Crusaders in their duties. I hurried off to let Salome know about the archangel.

On getting back to her palace I found her in the bedroom in a nightdress in a seductive pose. She held out her hand, beckoning me to sit beside her.

I gave her anxious look. 'I have been worried after I healed you in the convent,' I explained.

'That was some time ago in purgatory,' said Salome. 'We are now in heaven.'

'Yes, I know that, but you're confusing me about love-making.'

'What did archangel Raphael say?' Salome asked, hopefully.

'He's not there. Heaven knows when he's coming back,' I said.

'What are you confused about?' asked Salome, calmly.

'I told you,' I said, emphatically. 'Sex is not allowed in heaven.'

'Ask Our Lord,' said Salome. 'He adores women'

'The Lord is busy right now,' I said. 'He's been worshipped by the archangels the highest throne in heaven,' I said. 'I don't know if he's coming back.'

'You will have to take my word for it then,' she said, temptingly taking off her nightdress and inviting me to come nearer.

I looked at her soft lips and beautiful breasts and lo and behold I melted into her arms, kissing her passionately with an urge to seduce her.

Then I heard the voice of St. Michael saying: 'You're going to the devil if you fornicate.'

With that I immediately jumped off her. Shaking from head to foot, I pleading to God do not send me to hell.

'What's the matter with you,' said Salome, astonished with my outburst.

'You are re-infected,' I uttered. 'You are not healed of witchcraft. You will send me to hell in your devilish lust.'

'You're insane!' Salome protested. 'Love is what heaven is.'

'You call it love,' I said, indigently. 'Love doesn't come from the flesh. Love comes from the spirit, that's why we are resurrected to heaven.'

Salome dashed over to me and embraced me, holding me in her arms.

'I am completely yours in unconditional love,' she said, tears rolling down her cheeks. 'I am a soul-mate, but if you don't make love its fine. I'll be your sister, but don't send me away, please don't.'

I held her in my arms and kissed her tenderly. 'Let's be soul-mates and we'll never talk about sex again,' I said. 'We are sister and brother.'

Chapter 19

Witchcraft

The emergency meeting of the archangels was to delve into the possibility that witchcraft was entering heaven. St. Raphael implored the Senate to increase the Divine Crusaders to safeguard heaven.

'Before, we attached twelve angels to the far corner of heaven. That should be enough to thwart the demons,' said St. Michael, adamantly. 'They have done it before when the demons tried to get in.'

The archangels decided on a vote not to increase the Divine Crusaders as they excelled themselves on the driving out the demons.

I was called before the Senate to explain why witchcraft and demons should have entered heaven in the first place.

'Before, I was in the convent in purgatory and I healed the nuns of witchcraft whose mothers were witches in Salem on the earth. I have a nun sent to me by the Senate and she is my housekeeper. And now she is beckoning me to have affair with her. I came to the conclusion the nun was re-infected by witchcraft, now that sex is banished from heaven.'

'Are you in love?' St. Raphael asked.

'I am,' I stuttered.

'Then you should make love to her,' said St. Raphael, joyfully. 'Heaven is all about love.'

On hearing that the Senate ruled there is no case against Salome for being a witch.

'Then what about babies?' I asked.

'There's no reproduction in heaven,' St. Raphael said. 'Children that come to heaven are martyrs and they will grow into adults. There are no more babies. We're in heaven.'

'Then what you're saying is against St. Michael's rules,' I said, confused. 'He says that intercourse in heaven should not be allowed.'

'Love that counts,' said St. Raphael. 'Are you sure you're in love? You sensed that the nun was a witch. Are you sure?'

'I can't fathom is she's a witch or not,' I confessed, 'but I love her.'

'Then you should go back to her and pray to God that she won't be possessed.'

I thanked the archangel and set out to the far corners of heaven to see that the Divine Crusaders were watching out for infiltrators then headed back to my palace to confront Salome.

She was sitting by the pool eating strawberries and a glass of wine. I went up to her and kissed her on the cheek. 'How are you, Salome?'

'Did the meeting go OK?' she asked, concerned.

'I met St. Raphael and he said that we can make love,' I said, hesitantly.

Salome was enthralled. 'That's fantastic. I said St. Raphael is for women.'

I took Salome inside the house and up to the bedroom. I closed the curtains. Salome was undressing, taking off her stockings and undoing her bra.

'It's wonderful that we can make love at last!' said Salome, gushing. 'It's not a secret affair, but it's out in the open. We are in love.'

Salome lay down provocatively on the bed, submitting to my every need. She had an amazing figure, so sensual that I fondled her intimately.

I was about to proceed further when I heard a voice say:

'Don't do it,' said the voice, 'you're going to hell.'

It was archangel Michael.

I jumped off the bed and put my clothes on. Salome was aghast at my refusal to seduce her.

'What wrong with you?' she asked, indignantly.

'What's wrong with YOU?' I said, raising my voice. 'Tell me about your mother. Was she a witch?'

'Maybe,' said Salome. 'From the time you came to the convent when you healed the nuns you said she was a witch.'

'Are you re-infected? Are you possessed?' I asked, alarmed.

'Are you out of your mind?' said Salome, furiously. 'I have been healed ever since leaving the convent.'

My patience was running out and I paced the bedroom. If I was wrong I would repent, get on my knees but not to propose marriage. That would be unlawful in heaven.

Salome got out of bed and stood before me naked. She held me in her arms. 'It's in the past and now we're in heaven. Only peace and joy fill our hearts.'

'There is so much going on,' I said, hastily. 'I have to go now to see the Divine Crusaders. I'll be back soon.'

I set out to far corners of the heaven, not knowing if Salome was an angel - or a witch.

Chapter 20

Betrayal

I met with the Divine Crusaders near the border and they told me there was a battle with the demons who disguised themselves as Christians.

'What happened?' I asked, alarmed.

'We overcame them at side gate,' said John. 'There were legion of demons and they were led by a woman named Scarlet.'

That name rings a bell. Did I know her in Purgatory? That was it! Scarlet was a harlot virgin and sexually tantalized me before she lured to the Queen of the Harlots, Jezebel.

'Did you capture her?' I asked, alarmed.

'We did,' said John. 'She bound and gagged over by a tree.'

John led me over to the tree and there tied up was Scarlet. Before she was a harlot virgin and now she looked like an Amazon warrior out for blood and conquest. I took the gag off her.

'Why did you come here to heaven? Its God paradise'

'I came to conquer,' said Scarlet proudly. 'But your crusaders defeated them and they turned back, leaving me behind.'

'You are my prisoner now,' I said. 'Come with me.'

I led Scarlet to my palace and locked her in a dungeon. It is my responsibility as leader of the Divine Crusaders to impose a sentence on a beautiful woman, who lured me into a sexual encounter with the Jezebel and to send me to hell.

Scarlet was a demon of the highest order and now Salome, a nun who entered heaven, also a demon about to commit an affair with me, was re-infected by witchcraft.

Our Lord said that the chasm between heaven and hell cannot be crossed over. The rich man in hell can never be reached by the poor man in heaven. The poor man could never give a thirsty rich man below a drop of water to quench his thirst.

How can two women, revoking Our Lord's teaching, were allowed into heaven usurping God's kingdom?

It beggars belief!

Having locked Scarlet in the dungeon I went to find Salome and find out if indeed she was a witch from the horse's mouth. We met in the garden and she told me the truth.

'I lied to you,' said Salome. 'I have been cursed.'

Salome confessed when I told her about Scarlet having been crossed over to heaven to conquer the kingdom and arrested her and put her in a dungeon.

'What shall happen to us?' asked Salome, fearing the worst.

'I shall report it to archangel Michael,' I said.

'Then you won't execute us?' asked Salome, sobbing.

'He will decide.'

I put Salome and Scarlet in the dungeon and set off to see the archangel.

St. Michael admonished me when I arrived. 'You will suffer the consequences of the two women, witches who entered heaven. You were in charge.'

I hurried back to the dungeon, knowing my fate. Salome was standing by the gate. 'Are we going to be hanged?' she asked, like her mother was in Salem.

'No,' I said. 'I'm too am accused.'

'St. Michael issued a decree that Scarlet be sent to the under-world and Salome and I be sent to Purgatory,' I told them.

'Oh no,' cried Salome, and fainted in my arms.

'I'm going to be with Lucifer,' said Scarlet, smiling.

The Divine Crusaders took Scarlet to the gate and cast her into the eternal fire where Satan and the demons lived.

I was sent to Purgatory hoping that in time I might be forgiven for falling in love with Salome and be welcome back into heaven.

Chapter 21

Purgatory twice

Salome went back to the convent in Purgatory and I became a wandering monk from town to town. Salome was confronted by one nun, who had been infected by witchcraft.

'How long have you been infected?' Salome asked.

'I have been infected since the time of the Rapture. What brings you back to purgatory?' asks nun. 'Have you done something wrong?'

'I too have been re-infected,' said Salome, wiping a tear. 'Now that I'm here I don't think I'll be able to stand the trials ahead.'

'You rest awhile and I will bring you supper later,' said the nun, concerned.

Salome went to her cell and thought of how she was in purgatory for the second time. She was happy in heaven. What terrible crime she did commit? Was she is a witch, re-infected by her mother? It was her involvement in witchcraft changed the course of fortune to disaster? Was it sex?

Going over the times she was with me, it was love at first sight. She loved me and wanted to consummate our love. She remembered what archangel Michael said about sex. It was forbidden for humans not to reproduce in heaven. That was her downfall - she wanted a baby!

I was tempted to make love with Salome, her beautiful face

and long flowing golden hair, and her infectious smile. I was captivated by her feminine charms but it was my downfall being a Christian - fallen in love with a witch!

Now I was in purgatory for the second time.

Chapter 22

Paradise

In purgatory there is intense suffering like you've never witnessed on Earth. There is severe pain, mental anguish and the soul is suffering acutely like you were on death's door, like hell. It was severe torture.

I called out to God save me from soul from the trials of purgatory. After a time, peace entered my heart. Prayer saved my life, it was a blessing. Whatever life throws at you prayer is salvation, praying from the heart. I took a vow of silence and that way the only prayer words I spoke were from the spirit.

I spent a month surviving in the desert but the howling wind and sand made me suffer in silence. The sandstorm blew across the desert for a week and then it died down. It was time for me to go and visit the convent and Salome.

When I got to the convent Mother Superior led to her cell and thanked me for my prayers in driving away witchcraft before I went to heaven.

'My goodness, you are back in purgatory!' exclaimed the Mother Superior. You can see Salome. She is well considering after having gone through such an ordeal.'

I tentatively knocked on her cell and Salome was praying by the small altar by the window.

She looked up and seeing it was me jumped up and put her arms around me and hugged me. 'Oh, it's so good to see you after all these months. How have you been?'

'I'm OK, but what about you,' I asked, concerned. 'Are you well?'

'Yes, but I've thought about what brought me here,' said Salome. 'What about you? Have you thought about how you came to purgatory?'

'Yes, I have. It's all about my feelings for you,' I said, confessing. 'Because of my love for you, the archangels sent me to purgatory. Heaven doesn't allow a couple to have sex. That provokes jealousy. Love is to share among people and angels. Heavenly love is spiritual not material.'

'You were sent to purgatory because you'd love me?' Salome astonished.

'It's my downfall!' I blurted.

'Do you feel the same way,' she asked, anxiously. 'Do you love me?'

'I guess so,' I said, 'that's why I've come back.'

'Then let's make love.'

'You don't listen!' I said, infuriated. 'In heaven we are like angels and angels don't make love! That's simple. If you can get the message we can go back to heaven and be like the angels.'

'We can make love!' said Salome, defiantly. 'Archangel Raphael said so!'

'He's misinformed,' I said. 'He loved women to the point he put them on the pedestal and adored them. Our Lord said we are like angels in heaven and, like the angels, we abstained from sex. So, what it'll be then? We can make love in purgatory and go to hell or we can enter heaven with purity in our hearts?'

Salome collapsed in my arms in anguish and cried out: 'I'm confused. God is love and we are in love.'

I leaned over and kissed her on the cheek. Salome was ingrained for sexual reproduction in her DNA, like all earthly women.

Alas, the affair was over.

Chapter 23

Spiritual Pride

I set out on a road away from temptations and Salome. The sun came over from the mountains and I had a beautiful view of the green valley with its cedar trees and array of bluebells and daffodils.

The sheep were grazing in the valley but there wasn't a shepherd insight. The sheep had to fend for themselves in purgatory for they had to be independent and not rely on a shepherd.

I was the same, independent. I fell into the trap of over-confident and, low and behold, I was tempted by the devil! I marched through the valley with my chest out and ego soaring. I would enter heaven if it's the last thing I would do. Pride comes before a fall and I was fallen for a biggest temptation of all – spiritual pride!

On seeing a horse cart in the distance I stuck out my thumb and the driver, could you believe it, it was a woman with her buxom breasts and golden hair.

'Where are you going?' said the woman. 'I'm on way to farm yonder about a mile. I'm Rosie.'

'I'm going beyond the farm. I shall take a ride in your cart for my legs are weary,' I said. 'My name is Andy.'

About a mile on we came to a fork in the road and as we turned left there was a small farm on the right. 'Here we are,' said Rosie. 'Come in for supper, you look hungry.'

'I'm famished, I've not eaten for a few days,' I said, thankfully.

Rosie got off the cart and opened a door and we went into the kitchen.

I was grateful to the meal. She was about 30 years old and a widow.

'How did your husband die?' I asked, in sympathy.

'He was in an accident,' said Rosie. 'He was run over by a tractor five years ago and I had to survive alone living on the farm.'

'Why have you been brought to purgatory,' I asked, curiously.

'My husband died on the farm and I have been cast out because of my sins,' confessed Rosie, crying. 'I had an affair and now I'm in purgatory.'

'The Lord forgives,' I said, comforting her.

'I've lost my faith. It's another reason in here,' Rosie sobbed.

My heart went out to her, crying on her knees, full of self-loathing and low self-esteem. 'We are all fragile,' I said, picking her up off the floor and wiping her tears from her eyes.

'Hold me?' she pleaded.

I embraced her. The smell of her hair and soft skin aroused me as I held her tightly in my arms. She felt like a woman who needed a man, to take care of things, to look after the farm and comfort her.

Rosie led me into her bedroom and disrobed, taking off her bra and panties, stood naked before me. She has not made love for all those years and she urged me to take her forcefully and make her a complete woman.

'Please, let's talk for a minute,' I said, putting on her robe. 'There's something I should say about sex.'

'Let's make love and talk at the same time,' said Rosie,

stepping out of her robe and displaying a fine figure with perfect boobs.

'I have been cast out because of that,' I said, forlornly, looking at her body.

'What, talking?' asked Rosie.

'No, your body! Sex is forbidden in heaven,' I said, adamantly.

'No sex?' exclaimed Rosie. 'I don't believe in heaven.'

I looked at her naked body. 'I have been through that before with another woman in heaven. That's why I was cast out into purgatory. You said you don't believe in heaven? I've come from there!'

Rosie looked aghast and flung herself at me. She wrestled with me and got the better hand and low and behold she tied me to the bed. I pleaded with her to untie me and let me go. But she insisted I must do the deed before I went.

'I've tied you up because you didn't have balls when I was naked in front of you,' Rosie protested. 'Now it's my turn.'

I felt aroused when she got on top and kissed me all over. 'Don't do this,' I pleaded. 'I won't be going back to heaven if you have you way. Get off me.'

My pleading was to no avail. She grabbed my manhood and then she rocked back and forwards in a frenzied motion. She cried out in ecstasy as she reached orgasm.

I turned away in disgust. Hell awaits for sinners!

I left the farm where God's grace had forsaken me. I was weary and downhearted. All the deeds I had begun were fallen by the wayside, as if they were nothing. I have sinned against God, cast out again into purgatory. Fallen spirits never came back to heaven. It was the second death of souls.

There but for the grace of God go I. Mercy, forgiveness and

love was at the heart of Our Lord. I prayed for courage and God's forgiveness, courage to go on and reach the final destination, heaven. God forgive me for the sinful ways.

Can I ask God to enter heaven a second time? Trials await those to have harmed the Holy Spirit and test their patience, fortitude and faith.

I went into the desert depressed and alone. I attempted to built a make shift altar. For three days I knelt before the altar and prayed until a storm blew up and there before me was the archangel Raphael brandishing his wings.

'Your prayers have been heard,' said the archangel. 'Although I am not allowed to come down to fallen souls banished from heaven, but I take an exception. Your prayers have come from the heart. Come now, you will be taken heaven and begin again.'

'I am indebted to you archangel Raphael,' I said, bowing before him. 'Show me the way home.'

The archangel took me up out of purgatory to enter paradise, my true home.

Once again I was in eternity.

Chapter 24

Traitor

I entered New Jerusalem like I've never seen the city before. It has a magnificent golden dome with purple spires leading to a large plaza where girls were dancing to 'Rock and Roll Jesus'.

A multitude of people were clapping and having the time of their lives when I happened to notice a poor old man sitting by the stand. I went up to him and he looked up and said: 'I can't go any further.'

'What? You're in heaven,' I said, dumbfounded. 'You have eternal life.'

'Yes, but I can't go on,' said the old man, repeating.

'What's wrong?' I asked, compassionately.

'I don't know,' he said, muttering. 'All I know is I'm old and I can't go on.'

'Have you done anything in the past?' I asked.

'No, nothing I think of,' he said.

'Come with me. We can get some help from the archangel,' I said.

I called upon the archangel Raphael to come and attend to the old man who is sick of a malady. 'Rest awhile,' I said. 'The archangel will soon come.'

No sooner than I said that the archangel appeared. 'What's the matter?' said St. Raphael.

'I can't go on,' said the old man, repeating.

Archangel Raphael looked at the old man and turned to me and said: 'This man is an intruder, he was here by stealth. Cast him out.'

'He was an infiltrator?' I asked, amazed.

'Yes, and you were responsible for the Divine Crusaders but you were sent back to Purgatory. Now you are back you have a responsibility as head of the Divine Crusaders not to let any infiltrators break in. As I said before, heaven is protected by Divine Crusaders and the old man infiltrates because you were dismissed from your post. Paradise is for the heavenly hosts and angels and the throne of Our Lord. No one enters there but a pure heart. See to it that no-one enters other than Christians. You will see in the good time that you will be promoted. Farewell, my brother,' said archangel Raphael.

I turned to the old man but he was gone. On hearing the archangel speak of infiltrators, he was convicted in his heart and gone to the underworld.

I left New Jerusalem and I took up my post of head of the Divine Crusaders. How can I ever be tempted by a woman who seduced me, losing my job and sent to Purgatory? Never again! It was sheer folly and pride.

I headed out to the outer limits of heaven, keeping the peace in my home, where there was no more *femme fatales* to distract me from my duties, even Salome or Rosie.

I entered the lounge and there were two cheetahs to greet me. Animals were allowed in heaven and the cheetahs were so friendly, not so with *femme fatales*. They came up to and rubbed their noses at me purring. They wanted their food. I opened up a large tin of meat and they devoured it though they caught it.

I walked with the cheetahs in the garden and thought about

the Divine Crusaders, if they were up for the job and who would be replaced? Who is the traitor who sent me to purgatory? I will find out who is responsible for the devil's intrusion.

I met with the Divine Crusaders in the palace grounds and we went over the scene when the infiltrators, led by Scarlet, got over the wall to take over heaven.

'Who is the watchman who is looking out for infiltrators?' I asked.

'It is I,' said Judas, standing at the back.

'You didn't wake the other crusaders when the devils broke in?' I asked, pointing out that if the crusaders had been woken up they could have thrown out the infiltrators.

'When the demons broke in I was asleep,' said Judas. 'Forgive me.'

'How could be you asleep in when you are the watchman?' I asked, dumbfounded.

'I woke up when Scarlet threatened me with a sword,' said Judas. 'I was helpless.'

'You are dismissed from the crusaders,' I said. 'Go and get out of here.'

I turned to the crusaders and told them if there is one more disaster the whole Divine Crusaders would be fired. They looked at Judas as he departed. 'He should have woken us,' said a crusader.

The Divine Crusaders were ordered to their posts, listening out for the infiltrators, prominent among them was Scarlet. 'She is the Amazon woman who instigated the assault on heaven,' I said. 'Watch out for her.'

I went to my palace at the gate was a mystic holy man, with white hair flowing down and a beard, who said he had urgent message by Our Lord.

'Be thou vigilant,' said the mystic. 'If not thou will fall from grace.'

'I am vigilant,' I asserted. 'Thanks for your kindness.'

With that the mystic went off into the far away land never to see him again.

Why would the mystic know about such evil things in heaven for there is no disaster in heaven unless Satan and Scarlet had a hand in it? That was it! The mystic was right. Be vigilant for Scarlet!

She is the devil's advocate!

Chapter 25

Second assault

The Archangels were holding a Spiritual Symposium on the Heavenly Kingdom where Our Lord was presiding. The symposium was for all Christians. They put their cases forward, and I was one of them.

I addressed the forum. 'We have a problem with one of the devils. She is Scarlet, a warrior woman, who has led the infiltrators to enter heaven by force and now she's planning a second assault.'

Archangel Michael stood up and said I was the responsible for Divine Crusaders. 'You're in charge,' said the archangel. 'Was Scarlet cast out when you apprehended her the first time?'

'She was indeed cast out,' I said, vehemently.

'Then you've got no worries,' said the archangel. 'She's banished to the underworld.'

'I am worried,' I said. 'A holy man came to me telling that a prophecy was about to happen. The Divine Crusaders must be vigilant.'

'Of course they're vigilant,' said St. Michael. 'You trained them!'

A roar of laughter by the Christians echoed throughout the chamber.

'Yes, but the mystic told of the time would come when vigilant was put to the test,' I said. 'Scarlet was about to begin an assault on heaven.'

'Then you and the Divine Crusaders must stop them,' said the archangel. 'If you don't succeed you and the crusaders will be cast down and won't be coming back. You will be in hell eternally.'

All the Christians cried out to St. Michael saying the crusaders were caught out by the demons assault and would never happen again. I bowed to the Our Lord and the archangels. Scarlet and the demons would never reach heaven again and I pledged that the crusaders will return in triumph and never be called upon to evict the infiltrators.

Chapter 26

Salome pardoned

It was early in the morning when Our Lady Mary, the Queen of Heaven, strolled through the parks adoring the beautiful roses and the lake. It was a peaceful day but something had come up, namely Salome, who was in the convent.

Mary had got to know Salome on many occasions when she stayed for retreats, but she had been told she was cast out from heaven and into purgatory by no fault of her own. Mary had only seen the good in her it was unfair to evict her. She set out to restore Salome to paradise and be welcomed and serve in her palace.

Mary would go to her son, Our Lord, and explained that Salome should be sent to heaven because it unjust to send her to purgatory. 'How could that happen, sending her to purgatory? There must be a mistake,' Mary told Jesus.

'I will look into it mother,' said Our Lord.

I was summoned to heavenly court to explain my accusation that Salome was a witch.

St. Michael stood up and he addressed the court: 'The accused blames her of witchcraft and without any shred of evidence.'

I was called to the witness box. 'Salome was into sexual reproduction but there is no sex in heaven,' I said.

'She came on to me in a sexual way and I left her there in

purgatory for I was going to heaven. She was into procreation and heaven forbids it.'

'Where is the evidence she was into procreation?' asked St. Michael.

'From the horse's mouth, I said. 'She said so.'

'But there is no other witness,' said the archangel. 'You accused her of witchcraft. Where is the evidence?'

'I cast out the demon from her in the convent in purgatory,' I protested. 'She is a residual witch taken from her mother in the village of Salem, a haven of witches. You can ask the Mother Superior?'

'She's not here,' said St. Michael. 'Have you any other witnesses?'

I looked around. There was no one who could have seen me giving an exorcism at the convent in purgatory.

The case was dismissed and Salome was sent to reside at the palace of Our Lady to serve as the handmaid.

There were no witnesses that Salome was impure and seeking procreation. She deceived the whole court and wants to have a baby in paradise in Our Lady's palace!

Heaven forbid!

If only Mother Superior at the convent had been present, she would know that Salome was a witch.

I would go and see the Mother Superior. The nuns had entered heaven, and were staying in a convent, near New Jerusalem, after having been exorcised by me in purgatory.

I would go and find the truth if Salome was indeed a witch.

Chapter 27

Salome's return

The New Jerusalem was hive of activity, markets were flourishing, shops were opening and the new malls were jammed with shoppers. I made my way from the noise of the city to the peace of the convent.

I knocked on the receptionist door and the petite nun opened it and ushered me in. 'Mother Superior was tied up at the moment but I could wait in the reception,' the nun said, apologetically. She blossomed like an angel, having been exorcised by me at purgatory. She looked radiant.

'Do you know Salome?' I asked, out of curiosity.

'Yes, but she's been sent to purgatory,' said the nun, despondently.

'Salome is back,' I said, 'restored to heaven.'

'Praise God,' said the nun. 'The Mother Superior will see you now.'

I entered the Mother Superior office, a bright orange room with oil paintings depicting previous Popes. She greeted with a slight bowing of her head and said it was a present surprise to see me after I exorcised the nuns.

'I have come to see you regarding Salome,' I said.

'I received a phone call,' said Mother Superior proudly. 'She been back to heaven and is the handmaid to Our Lady.'

'My understanding is that Salome has deceived the heavenly

court and she wants to conceive a child.'

'That is the wish of all women who come to paradise, but that's impossible. Women don't give birth because they are like angels. We have spiritual bodies.

'But Salome wants to make love,' I said. 'That is impossible in heaven,'

'You are quite right,' said the Mother Superior. 'But for women who struggle for perfection, they will make love in an exception. In time, they enter into God's love of perfection.'

'You mean Salome is right,' I said. 'She can make love?'

'If she has recanted her vows of nun and she can make love, in an exception. It brings closer relationships' said Mother Superior.

'She's a witch,' I said, horrified.

'But you healed her by exorcism,' said Mother Superior.

'Yes, but she a recidivist witch' I protested. 'Her mother, a witch from Salem, contacted her after I perform exorcism and made her recurring witch.

'Heaven forbid!' said the Mother Superior.

'You weren't at the heavenly court,' I said. 'You were witness to exorcism but you didn't attend, why not?'

'I was ill at the time,' said the mother. 'You must go to Our Lady and tell her what you told me. I must go now, its prayer time for the nuns.'

I thought about what Our Lady would say if I tell Salome is a witch. She is employed by Our Lady as handmaiden and if she thinks Salome's a witch and then two possible outcomes. The first is Our Lady dismisses Salome and sends her to the heavenly court where sentence imposed. The second is that Salome would deny she's a witch and Our Lady sends me to the outer of heaven, where I would be ostracized.

I wrestled with my conscience on how I would approach Our Lady. It seems Salome has the upper hand. She is a handmaid and what goes in the palace stays in the palace. She would be part of palace's gossip, albeit whispering in Our Lady's ear!

Salome, to all intents on purpose, has won.

I flew to the palace of Our Lady, a majestic mansion on the lake, near New Jerusalem, and arrived in an instant, such was the means of travelling celestial.

Upon arriving I introduced myself to the butler as Chief of the Divine Crusaders, Security of the Heavenly Kingdom. I was escorted into the parlour and introduced to Our Lady, Mary Mother of God.

'Your highness I have come on a delicate matter concerning your maid servant, Salome.'

'Yes, what is it now?' asked Our Lady, calmly.

'I have been informed she is a witch,' I said, with conviction.

'A witch!' cried out Mary. 'A witch does not exist in heaven. What makes you say that?'

'We were in purgatory together and I exorcised her from witchcraft and now she wants to have sex with me and so I refused because sex is not allowed in heaven,' I protested. 'She is a witch.'

'You misunderstood,' said Mary. 'Sexual union is allowed in heaven in exceptional circumstances to bring couples together. You exorcised Salome in purgatory and now she is cured and in paradise.'

'Can I see Salome?'

'If you wish,' said Our Lady, 'she is in the garden.'

I went to the garden, a magnificent lawn with roses and

geraniums and swans swimming in the pond. At the far end was Salome sitting on a park bench feeding the peacocks.

Salome glanced upward and on seeing me, said: 'How are you? I haven't seen for awhile.'

'I'm fine,' I said, noticing her blonde locks and figure. 'I've been to see Our Lady.'

'What about,' said Salome, getting up.

'It's about you,' I said. 'Come, let's go for a walk.' My thoughts were of Our Lady saying 'exceptional circumstances', making love was allowed.

We strolled through the garden and by the side of the oak tree I took Salome in my arms. Forgetting about the arguments we had, I kissed her tenderly on the cheeks. She melted in my arms. It was a long kiss and it was overwhelming to the point Salome had to pull away.

'My, you got carried away,' said Salome. 'You said sex isn't allowed, is it?'

'I was wrong,' I confessed. 'Sex in heaven is allowed in exceptional circumstances!'

'That's right. Come, there's a cosy hide-away so no one can see,' beckons Salome.

We took a path leading to a small cottage where the game-keeper was away on business.

'How come you've changed your mind?' asked Salome as we arrived at the cottage.

'Guess I was foolhardy,' I admitted. 'Our Lady put me in place,'

'You took awhile,' said Salome. 'Now take me and do what-ever you want.'

Salome was standing by a sofa and promptly undressed,

taking her bodice off and the stockings and panties.

She looked beautiful her golden locks hanging over her shoulders and beckoning me to come closer.

I turned and locked the door. Salome was in bed in a provocative position inviting me to seduce her from behind.

'I thought you prefer a missionary position,' I said, alarmed.

'We can do what we like,' said Salome. 'We are in heaven.'

'There is something I want to talk about?' I said, interrupting her.

'Not now,' Salome said, anxious to be impregnated. 'What is it?'

'Have you had recurring thoughts about witchcraft?' I said, questioningly.

'Sometimes,' admitted Salome. 'But that was years ago in purgatory.'

Sometimes means **now** for a witch. Witchcraft would entirely destroy an angel by force in an instant.

'When did you last have thoughts about witchcraft in heaven?' I asked, bluntly.

'I don't know,' said Salome. 'It goes away.'

'I have not healed you at all,' I said. 'You are under the influence of your mother from Salem.'

'How dare you say that?' Salome protested. 'You healed me at the convent when I was in purgatory.'

'You said that you had recurring thoughts about witchcraft in heaven,' I said, accusing her.

'I meant purgatory,' said Salome, protesting. She climbed off the bed and got dressed. 'Now get out of the palace before I call Our Lady.'

I left with reservations. What terrible things may happen

to heaven if she delves in witchcraft? For she knows being a witch what will happen next - Lucifer will usurp the kingdom of heaven!

Chapter 28

Virgin Crusaders

The temperature in heaven was warm every day of the year because sun is shining 24 hours a day and why all people do not sleep. They are worshipping God all the time.

In New Jerusalem the heavenly hosts were about to hold a forum. The first agenda was what to do with an influx of women, about 1,000 virgins, who entered heaven by rapture.

I was promoted to Director of Eastern Hemisphere and my first assignment was to take the women to the Eastern Hemisphere and provide for them a huge mansion. It was for all intents and purposes a harem, for they were all virgins and no other men would be there apart from me and eunuch servants.

I entered the mansion on the outskirts of the eastern part of the kingdom with 500 rooms and a swimming pool and leisure centre. The women, teenagers up to thirty, each shared a room overlooking oranges and lemons trees. It was paradise.

The women dressed in their swimwear were surprised by the huge mansion with its golden turrets and oval shaped windows and delighted by the spacious rooms.

In the afternoon, escorted by the eunuchs to form a parade, I address the women, announcing that in the eastern Hemisphere they formed a unique section of heaven.

'You women are about to form a virgins' territory known as the Virgin State. No men must come here. For you are about to become the Virgins of the Eastern Hemisphere and whole purpose of being here is to worship God.

'You will be safe here for you are in paradise. Any intrusions by the devil I will deal with the Divine Crusaders.'

A formidable woman, Ophelia, came forward and introduced herself as a war heroine from Earth. 'I am the leader of the virgins and we can deal with any intrusions,' she said with authority.

Ophelia was a striking woman with blonde hair, a slim figure and big breasts. On Earth she survived the sun and nuclear explosions by Rapture along with the virgins.

I took her to my palace and welcome her achievements with a glass of wine. I explained my job as director of the Eastern Hemisphere. She asked what the responsibilities of women were, apart from praising Our Lord. Then she asked:

'The virgins don't want Divine Crusaders as security, and why are they parading around in bikinis, you may ask. I will tell you?'

She said that women are born naked and die naked and they are resurrected naked. 'We as women love our natural bodies. Bikinis are to tantalize men for they are still virgins.'

'You mean they don't be virgins, like the nuns,' I said, dismayed.

'Women were virgins before rapture and were called for marriage and children.'

'Women in heaven don't marry,' I said. 'They are like angels.'

'I know. It's just that women by their nature long to have children. You must know that?' said Ophelia, showing her cleavage.

I nodded in agreement. Our Lady and Salome confirmed it.

'How come you don't want security of Divine Crusaders?' I asked, puzzled.

'We have the Virgin Crusaders. They have a black belt in karate and a force to be reckoned. They can deal with the invaders,' said Ophelia.

'You don't say,' I said, surprised at what women will do.

'The virgins protest that eunuchs dwell at the mansion. 'Where are the men?' she said. 'Virgins want romance.'

All I need is thousand virgins want to be deflowered by the Divine Crusaders and all hell would break out. As Director of Eastern Hemisphere I would put a stop to that. Discipline is vital if we keep our heavenly borders secure.

The Virgin Crusaders must show self-restraint to protect their borders, if not morality would break down and the borders would be invaded. There is one possible way in which the virgins would be satisfied. Satisfying them with love!

I would be their source of affection, the only male in the virgin mansion.

But the virgins would cry out for men to seduce them and take away their virginity and make them a whole woman. In heaven a soul must be at peace and that why marriage is forbidden. The virgins must know that and be satisfied with my affection and God's love.

'You must call the women to form a parade and I will address them and tell what to do,' I said, sternly.

Ophelia stood up. 'I have told them before they are like angels. You said that your affection would satisfy their cravings, we'll see. Virgins are really randy. Take my word for it. I'm one of them.'

The parade was formed with one thousand virgins in their

scanty bikinis eying up the Director of the Eastern Hemisphere. They stood at ease showing off their figures.

I inspected them in ten rows deep. Temptation was all around for they were beautiful and stunning each and every one of them.

Why so many virgins were so horny? Did Salome have anything to do with this? I set out to find the truth after I addressed them.

'You have come from Earth by way of Rapture and praise God. I met your leader Ophelia and welcome your new home in Eastern Hemisphere.

'I have been told that you are virgins. Blessed are you for your virginity. They will hold a place in Heaven, like the nuns. However, it has been called to my attention that you are protesting about eunuchs.

'I make myself perfectly clear that you do not converse with other men for that leads to you falling from grace. I have been told that your needs are fulfilled by affection. Come to me for spiritual comfort, not going off to copulate with my Divine Crusaders, for that will lead to disaster. You are like angels and not be tied down with earthly attachments.'

I address the twelve Virgin Crusaders. 'I want to thank you for a courageous endeavour protecting your women and the hemisphere. We can talk about your duties.'

The virgin women clapped and sang alleluias as I was escorted by the twelve Virgin Crusaders to my palace.

The women entered my palace with their skimpy bikinis, a sight for lusty men on Earth. I set about finding the truth and if Salome was at the centre of sorcery in finding males to seduce and send back to purgatory.

After hearing of their duties the virgins went back to their palace, all except one. She was Fiona, who stayed behind wanting to tell a secret.

'I want you informed there is a secret among the virgins,' said Fiona, whispering.

'What's the secret?' I asked. 'It is about Salome?'

'If I tell, you'll do something for me?' asks Fiona.

'What?'

'Will you make love to me?' pleaded Fiona.

I looked at her. She was beautiful and gorgeous with a fine figure and golden hair hanging down to her shoulders. She waved her eyelashes. If I agreed to seduce her then I would lose my job and about to be cast out.

'Tell me about the secret first,' I said, hesitantly.

'Will you make love to me?' she repeated. 'It would fulfil my needs.'

'What are you needs?' I asked.

'I want to be a real woman,' she moaned. 'I'm still a virgin.'

I looked at her again with sultry pose and longing to be seduced.

'Has Salome has anything to do with this?' I said, firmly.

'Who's Salome?' she asked.

'She's a witch or an angel, I know not,' I said. 'She now resides at the palace serving Our Lady, Mother of God.'

'A woman came to the palace, I know not where she came from and asked to speak with Ophelia in secret,' said Fiona.

'You must find out the name of the woman,' I urged. 'It's imperative.'

'Then you will make love to me?'

'We'll see.'

Fiona went back to the palace to find out the woman who

came to see Ophelia. The next day she came back to my palace to tell me the news.

'It was Salome,' said Fiona. 'She told Ophelia that she was on a secret mission. That's all I've heard.'

'I knew it was Salome! But you've got to find out the secret mission then I'll comfort you.'

'I don't want you to comfort me. I want you to make love to me,' said Fiona, earnestly.

'You are a virgin and I told you before virgins are honoured in heaven,' I said. 'Do you want to me to deflower you? You would lower yourself and be without grace and me too.'

'I am in heaven and do what I want,' said Fiona, defiantly.

'Yes, but you are like the angels,' I said. 'But they never reproduce.'

'Our Lady said we can make love,' said Fiona. 'I heard it from Ophelia.'

'I know it is on special circumstances! But not in the virgins' mansion, it would send my Divine Crusaders back to purgatory! You heard from Ophelia that Salome was the instigator?'

'But she got it from Our Lady,' said Fiona. 'We can make love - that's what heaven is, making love!'

'No, it's about purity and the love of God,' I said. 'That way we can be united with Our Lord.'

Fiona turned and put her hands up to heaven. 'If we don't make love, what is the point?' and stormed off to the virgin's mansion furious.

Chapter 29

Sorcery

The controversy over whether the virgins should take male lovers was high on the agenda. I would take it to the highest place in heaven, the throne of Our Lord. He would pronounce wisdom on the matter, as King Solomon did all those years ago on earth.

I didn't have enough evidence though to prove Salome was a witch. She was the instigator in the downfall of the Eastern Hemisphere by sexual corruption. But I did piece together some evidence that Salome was behind the sorcery that infiltrated the palace and she conspired with Ophelia to commit affairs.

I put my evidence to the archangel Michael and if he decides that the case go before the heavenly council, presiding over by Our Lord. 'Witchcraft does not enter heaven,' said the archangel. 'You say she is a witch?'

'Salome was a nun in purgatory and before she came to heaven. I exorcised the demon in her and now has come back to haunt the hemisphere of witchcraft. I have a thousand virgins and Salome wants to trick them by sorcery to have affairs with my Divine Crusaders,' I said, protesting.

'What proof to do have?' asked St. Michael. 'I cannot put your case to the council when there is no evidence.'

'Salome is a recidivist witch. She got it from her mother.

The witchcraft was evident in the time of Salem and she spread it while she was in the convent in purgatory. The evidence is that I exorcised the nuns,' I said, with conviction.

'But that was in purgatory,' said the archangel. 'She has been cured by you own admission and now she's in heaven with Our Lady. I cannot put your case to the council. I'm sorry but you'll have more evidence than that.'

I went back to my palace infuriated. Salome is to be caught in the act of sorcery if it means hell or high water!

Chapter 30

Queen of the Jews

Beauty in the eyes of the beholder, poet John Keats said. Yet beauty comes from God. It takes on forms of creation, like the planets and the woman Eve, the first woman. Beauty is the spiritual dimension of God's purpose and culminates in love of humans, particularly so when it comes to women. Take for instance the artists, who managed for centuries on earth to capture the beauty of the women, like Raphael, Leonard de Vinci and Botticelli.

The artists' inspiration comes from the spiritual beauty of God, not the beholder. The artist sees in her classical features, high cheekbones, swan-like neck, Roman nose and doe-like eyes. All come from God.

Now in heaven we are spiritual bodies and we all have the beauty of creation, particularly so in women who have the gifts of loyalty and grace. The number one is Our Lady, the Mother of God. She personifies the feminine qualities all women to be loyal, be the servant of God, humble and faithful. That is what women should be, not like the earthly feminists. They are out for themselves and women's downfall. They should be at home serving their husbands and children. That is what God made them for, to rear children and obey their husbands.

A woman like that I met on a mission to New Jerusalem. Her name is Grace, a heavenly name, full of elegance and beauty.

She was welcome to paradise by the archangels and led her into a royal palace where she was consecrated Queen of the Western Hemisphere.

At lunch I was introduced to her. Grace was tall, high cheekbones and green eyes with red hair flowing down her waist and a golden dress with a Empress bust-line.

'Congratulations on your appointment,' I said, bowing. 'When are you leaving for the Western Hemisphere?'

'Thank you,' said Grace, gracefully. 'I shall be going today.'

'What are your duties in the Western Hemisphere?'

'I am the Queen of the Western Hemisphere and my responsibility is the security and protection of all that live there,' said Grace.

'I am the Director of the Eastern Hemisphere,' I said. 'I would like to see the western hemisphere, if it pleases you.'

'You're welcome,' said Grace. 'You might disapprove of what you see.'

'You're the Queen, I can't disapprove,' I said, gracefully.

The Queen and I went to the Western Hemisphere, a vast open plain as far as the eyes could see, and wasting no time she led me into the arena where six million souls were saved.

'Who are they?' I asked.

'They are Jews from the Holocaust. Six million gassed by the Nazis and saved by the Rapture. They are now at home and I shall be their Queen.'

Spread out before me were the Jews perished by the death camps. They were all beautiful, radiant in the prime of their lives, and praised God for saving their lives. They were at peace in paradise.

'Such a sight could down in history but they were in heaven

now and history is a thing of the past. Thank be to God,' I said, astonished. 'Did the Jews convert to Jesus?'

'Yes, they were saved by the blood of Christ, taken up by the Rapture,' Grace said with conviction. 'I must welcome them to western hemisphere.'

The Queen stood before them and confessed that she was a Jew in the holocaust. 'I was in Auschwitz concentration camp and taken by the Rapture into paradise. Brothers and sisters, you died a martyr's death and you were raised up and now have a spiritual body which will last forever. There is no fear, for fear is cast out by love. Everlasting peace will be yours and you will enjoy paradise. The prophecy has come true. Welcome your new home.'

The Jews stood up and sang Alleluias, Alleluias. But the leader, Samuel, said: 'We are blessed in coming here, but we are not really Jews anymore.

'We are like the angels. You come to us from Auschwitz, heaven be praised, for you are our queen.'

The Queen stood before them and praised for their courage and faith. 'You my brothers and sisters are free. Now go forth into eternity and fill your lives with happiness.'

Chapter 31

Medical experiments

The Queen invited me to her city in the heartland of the Western Hemisphere, named after Nefertiti, the Egyptian princess, the most beautiful woman on earth. Grace adored Nefertiti and she wanted to preserve her name.

'My, you have an enormous palace,' I said, walking through the immense lounge. 'Do you have servants, like Our Lady?'

'I have no-one,' said Grace. 'I want to be free.'

'Tell me about your time in Auschwitz,' I asked, inquisitively.

Grace showed me an arm where the numbers were etched in black.

'I have a spiritual body but the number is always there. The Nazis were counting the Jews. I was fifteen years old at the time. I was sent to Dr. Mengele for medical experiments. He undressed me and although it was medical experiments he sexually abused me,' said Grace, lowered her eyes.

'Did he hurt you?' I said.

'There was one medical experiment where he put his hand up my vagina and he was thrusting until he had a fist inside of me. It was agony. He tore at my hymen. He took my virginity away. There were other experiments which I don't remember.'

'Was there anyone to help you,' I said, concerned.

'There was no-one to help me and that is why I have no servants. What about you? You have servants?'

'I have eunuchs,' I said. 'There are 1000 virgins at the eastern hemisphere and they look after them.'

The Queen was shocked at the amount of virgins there was. The trauma of losing ones virginity with heinous Dr. Mengele was evident.

I looked at her and she had a tear in her eye. She was upset what happened to her even though she survived Auschwitz and is now in paradise.

'Did you forgive him?' I asked, for forgiveness was at the heart of being a true Christian.

'Yes, but eventually,' said Grace. 'But he will go to God's judgement.'

'Is he in hell?'

'God will decide.'

We walked through the lounge and out through the refectory into the garden and sat down by the pool. The Queen was silent and pensive, dealing with the trauma of her childhood. I held her arm out and looked at the Nazi numbers. They were seven digits, the number of Jews exterminated in the death camps.

'The numbers are evil and now that I'm in paradise we're free,' said Grace, shedding a tear.

I held her hand out of compassion and told her that we're secure in paradise. 'We have the security in the Divine Crusaders watching out for the intruders in the eastern hemisphere. Our borders were invaded by the demons recently.'

The Queen was horrified. 'The demons invaded heaven?' asked Grace, appalled. 'What happened?'

I explained that the infiltrators, led by the Amazon warrior Scarlet, were thwarted at the border by the Divine Crusaders in an attempt to overthrow the kingdom.

'Why on earth will they do that?' said the Queen. 'This is heaven.'

'You know why the archangel Michael defeated Satan?' I said. 'Satan was jealous of God and is about to usurp his kingdom when archangel Michael banished him and sent him to hell. That is why you must have security for the Western Hemisphere, not knowing when the demons are coming to attempt to overthrow the kingdom.'

'The Jews are not fit for armed combat, seeing that what they have suffered,' said the Queen, anxiously.

'I will see to it,' I answered. 'You and the Jews will be safe. I will instruct the Divine Crusaders to look after them.'

The Queen smiled and glanced over to the swans gliding in the lake. 'It is peaceful here,' she said, walking by my side. 'Do you know the infiltrators you mentioned?'

I mentioned Scarlet. 'She was devious and I suspect she was influenced by witchcraft, as well as Salome.'

'Salome? Was she the one who is handmaid to Our Lady?'

'Yes, I've meet before a long time ago when she was a nun in purgatory,' I said. 'She was healed of witchcraft before she came to heaven, but I suspect that Salome, being a recidivist witch, manifests at another time.'

'Do you mean Salome is a witch in heaven?' said the Queen, shocked.

'I suspect that is the case,' I said.

'If he is a witch then it must be she is a good witch for she is the handmaid of Our Lady,' said Grace, appalled by the accusation. 'Perhaps she comes from the Druids, who practice witchcraft and praises nature.'

'But Salome comes from Salem, the witches in North

America, where her mother was hanged with 13 other witches. She was in the convent where I exorcised her and other nuns from witchcraft,' I said, earnestly.

'You are an exorcist?' said the Queen, surprised.

'I was a consecrated monk and it was given to me by the Holy Spirit,' I said. 'I exorcised the seven nuns at the convent, Salome being one of them.'

The Queen apologised and said exorcism was a gift from God. 'I will visit Our Lady and find out if Salome is witch or not,' said the Queen. 'Goodbye, 'til we meet again.'

Chapter 32

Queen meets Our Lady

Queen Grace escorted by the two handmaidens arrived at Our Lady's palace with angels blowing trumpets as she walked up the aisle.

Our Lady, the Mother of God, sat upon the throne beckoning her to come forward. Queen Grace, with her red hair flowing and green sparkled eyes, curtsied before Our Lady.

'I welcome you to this palace,' said Our Lady. 'You are the Queen of the Western Hemisphere. What can I do for you?'

'My lady, I am honoured to be the Queen of the Western Hemisphere, ruling over six million Jews gassed in concentration camps and the saved by the rapture. We honour Jesus and you for giving us eternal life.'

'I thank you but my son resurrected you to eternal life. I'm only his mother,' said Our Lady. 'What may I ask have you come for?'

'You have a handmaiden, Salome, in your care,' said Queen Grace. 'Can I see her?'

'Of course,' said Our Lady. 'She's in the garden.'

The Queen bowed and went into the garden, the most beautiful array of flowers and orange and apple trees she had ever seen.

There in the shade of an apple tree was Salome watering plants. She stood up, and recognising Grace as Queen she curtsied, well aware she was coming to see her.

'Now let me guess.' the Queen said. 'You knew of my appointment with Our Lady?'

'It was the Director of the Eastern Hemisphere, Andy. He was a monk in the past life and he told me.'

The Queen smiled and sat down by the apple tree. 'How long you have known Andrew?'

'For ages,' answered Salome, 'going back when we met in purgatory.'

'When were you in purgatory?'

'I was in a convent taking a vow as a nun,' said Salome. 'That was about a few years back. Why do you ask?'

Grace paused for a moment. 'Was Andrew at the convent?'

'I met him there,' said Salome.

'Did the nuns go through exorcism carried out by him?'

'Did he tell you?' Salome asked. 'It was ages ago. He was a monk gifted with the Holy Spirit and he healed the nuns because they were sick.'

'What pray tell was the nuns' sickness?' the Queen ask, concerned.

'Witchcraft,' confessed Salome. 'It was a long time ago and the nuns were healed and came to heaven.' She looked into the Queen eyes. They were consoling and sympathetic. Grace was indeed the most beautiful woman in heaven, apart from Our Lady.

Salome was smitten by Grace and embraced her with a kiss. Confronted by the warm affection, the Queen on the contrary enjoyed it and returned with a tender kiss. So much so, the two beautiful women in paradise, what appears to be plutonic relationship, ended up in romance.

Sorcery, or so it seems, had entered paradise.

I found out they were lovers when the Queen Grace returned to my palace. She came in with rose coloured cheeks and beaming smile.

'I found Salome not a witch, said Grace. 'On the contrary, she's an angel. I find her enchanting and full of love.'

'Salome is your lover?' I said, alarmed. 'But she's a witch.'

'You are bewitched!' said the Queen, remonstrating. 'You don't know how two women can love each other? You're a misogynist. You hate lesbians. I am the Queen and I'll have the thrown out of heaven.'

'Hell or purgatory?' I asked. 'I'm not a misogynist, as you so rudely pointed. In fact love women. I just can't imagine that you, the most beautiful woman in the world, could ever fall for a devious Salome.'

'You don't know what love is,' said Grace. 'Love is pure, like Salome. Now go and recruit the Divine Crusaders for my borders. Shame on you.'

Chapter 33

Eternal Love

I arrived at Eastern Hemisphere and I asked for volunteers to crusade for the borders of Western Hemisphere. There was none. It seems my accusation of witchcraft had been spread throughout the region.

But where can I find recruits to secure the Western borders and relieve me not going to purgatory as the Queen threatens. The Queen has the power to evict anyone who goes against her wishes and disobeys.

I sat in my palace and prayed for a miracle. All around me was a deep sense of loneliness. I can't go on as a director for I was not up for heavenly duties. Then, all of a sudden, like a thunderbolt, there appeared before the archangel Raphael.

'I listened to your prayers,' said Raphael. 'You go to the Queen and tell her that you'll unite Eastern and Western Hemispheres. There will be a union and all will be one.'

'I how do that?' I asked.

'Marry her,' said the archangel. 'The mission will be accomplished.'

'But Our Lord said no marriages exist in heaven,' I protested.

'It's not the same as earthly marriages,' said the archangel. 'We have what's called the State of Eternal Love. It's called a union. It's your mission,' said Raphael.

'But our Queen has a partner,' I said, sadly. 'She is in a

relationship with Salome.'

'Don't worry,' said the archangel. 'All will be well.'

'What about the recruits the Queen wants?' I asked.

'All will be well.'

With that he disappeared in a trail of white smoke, leaving me with a mission about to fulfil. What if she repels my romantic advances? What if she casts me out for disobeying her orders and sent me to purgatory or even hell?'

That amounts to a spiritual test, for what is carried out on earth by all Christians under trial, so it is for heaven. I must listen to what the archangel said: 'All will be well'. If a miracle is about to happen, then I must obey the archangel Raphael.

I went upstairs to get ready for my *fete accompli,* for if the Queen repels my romantic advances I will pay the penalty - eviction from heaven!

I put on my golden armour on, which I preserve for a state occasion, and for my sword admired by the Queen for its chivalry and security of her borders.

I'm a soldier at heart when it comes to romancing the Queen, for she being a woman, surrenders to a uniform. I must take care of Salome, for she is my *bête noire.* She must not interfere in my romancing Queen.

I approached the Queen's palace with my stallion and entered the garden where Salome was pruning the roses.

'Are you not serving Our Lady?' I said, greeting her.

Surprised at my intrusion, Salome stood up and said she was here to help for the Queen, for the gardener was away. 'I've come to some business with the Queen,' I said. 'Will you wait here for me? I shan't be long.'

'Are you proposing to me?' said Salome, optimistically.

I entered the palace and announced that I was there to see the Queen on official business. I was escorted to the waiting room and I sat wondering what on earth I would say to convince that I was a potential suitor.

Nothing came until I felt the surge in my body, a spiritual energy, to the point had the power to transform a woman's heart. It was the same energy that I exorcised the nuns at the convent all those years ago in purgatory.

On entering her suite I bowed to the Queen and laid before my plans to woe her with unrelenting romance. With that she recoiled and fainted.

I stepped forward and placed my hands upon her and recited a poem I had written, 'Ode to thee my darling Grace'. She sat up and looked at me with adoring smile, and lo and behold, she kissed me. My poem had effect on her, wooing her with total affection. It's not a kiss you would expect from a relative or even someone close to you. It was a full blown kiss, passionately and wantonly.

With the gift of exorcism, I cast out of the Queen the wiles and sorcery of Salome she had inflicted.

Grace turned to me with a tender embrace. She loved me from that moment on. The most beautiful woman in the world after Nefertiti, the Queen was my soul mate.

Chapter 34

Love betrayed

The Queen and I entered New Jerusalem and before Our Lord and Mary, Mother of God, to declare our mutual love for each other. The Union of Eternal Love was declared by Our Lord and trumpets echoed round the aisle and the angels dance in glory.

Now that the Queen and I are betrothed, the East and West Hemispheres are one State. The Divine Crusaders will patrol all the borders between east and west for the security of heaven and for the security of the Queen and her subjects.

The Queen and I were raised upon a high platform and angels danced around us with their trumpets blaring and the crowds shouting. It was all too much for the Queen, unsteady on her feet, was about to faint.

I called my stallion and we got away for the peace and quiet of the country. It was conducive to the peaceful love we shared as opposed to the trumpets blasting and shouting crowds.

I arrived at the country estate with my Queen, revitalized from the ride. We went inside and I lifted up Grace with strong hands as I carried her into the palace in the old-fashion way, taking the bride over the threshold.

She looked stunning as I placed her down on to the sofa. Her dress was up over her thighs and her silk panties and suspenders were showing.

I looked again how beautiful she was. I held her in my arms and caressed her soft breasts and thighs. Overwhelming passion took over me and I made love like never before as she murmured in my ear. She came several times as I held her tightly, her every muscles contracted, shuddering with every orgasm.

'I love you,' she murmured again, 'I love you.'

Our romance blossomed with every passionate embrace until one morning she received from a letter from a lady. That lady was indeed my first wife. She said I was a bigamist.

'Do you have another wife?' the Queen asked, angrily.

'That was in the past life,' I explained.

'How long ago?' she asked.

'Ages ago, we had an earthly marriage.'

The Queen stood up and said she was going to meet the lady and know the truth.

'I not have sex in heaven with this woman,' I said, innocently, 'because we are like angels.'

'You have sex with me!' retorted the Queen.

'But you are different,' I said. 'You are of royal blood and besides we can't reproduce. It's not permitted in paradise.'

The Queen was adamant and she hired a stagecoach to take her to Sarah.

What would Sarah say to the Queen? If she told the truth it would be my downfall. I would be sent to purgatory or to hell!

Chapter 35

Grace

The Queen arrived at Sarah's country house on the outskirts of New Jerusalem. Sarah was informed of her arrival by an angel. She was delighted by the Queen's visit and got the tea and cakes out.

The Queen, taking off her wedding dress after she was told her that I had another wife, wore a red dress with gold buttons, about to confront her rivalry. Introducing herself as Grace, the Queen confronted Sarah and asked if she was married.

'Yes, but an earthly marriage,' said Sarah. 'Now in heaven, we don't marry. We are like the angels.'

The Queen sat down and thought about what Sarah said. 'I got married,' said Grace, matter-of-factly. 'The ceremony is the Union of Everlasting Love. It is for lovers to want to be together. Who is your husband?'

'His name is Andy. Do you know him?' asked Sarah.

'He's MY husband,' said Grace, adamantly.

'You're the third wife,' said Sarah, sighing.

'The THIRD?!' screamed Grace, outraged. 'He said he was a monk?!'

'He became a monk after the earthly marriages were over,' said Sarah. 'You said that the ceremony was a union. His vows of being a monk are over when he married you in heaven. He has you now. Have no fear.'

The Queen thanks Sarah and wished her the best. 'Anything I could do for you let me know,' she promised.

All her fears of adultery were gone and the Queen went away with Salome on her mind. She would tell Salome that the relationship was over with her and that she would find another lover.

Chapter 36

Menage-a-trios

The sun was bearing down on the bikini girls around the pool in the Queen's palace. In the garden was Salome, who had finished pruning the roses, and was about leave when the Queen enters.

Salome went up to Grace and greeted her with a kiss, but the Queen recoiled and said she wanted a word in private. Salome took her towel and dried her hair as she followed her into the lounge. 'What's the matter?' asked Salome.

'If you haven't heard, I was married yesterday,' said the Queen. 'It was all a bit sudden, but he swept me off my feet.'

'How could you?' said Salome, perplexed. 'You were in love with me!'

'*C'est la vie*,' answered Grace. 'Whatever will be, will be.'

'Who is this person who swept you off your feet?' said Salome, angrily.

'You know him very well,' replied the Queen. 'He met you in the convent in purgatory.'

'Well I never,' said Salome. 'You married Andy?'

'He's charming,' said Grace. 'You do know that he was married on Earth? That is all forgotten now he is heaven.

'I, as the Queen of the Western Hemisphere and Andy, director of the Eastern Hemisphere, by union in an act of love, we have merged the two hemispheres.'

'That's amazing. He is charming,' confessed Salome. 'I too am quite enamoured by his presence. I wish you all the best. I would love to come and meet you and your husband sometime.'

'It would be delighted. You're so understanding,' said Grace

'The two people I love are you and your husband,' said Salome, hoping that Grace would share their intimate romance between three of us. The problems are solved, thought Salome, between Grace and Salome by *ménage-a-trios* with me.

Salome said goodbye to Grace and left the palace to return to Our Lady's estate. Grace was against sorcery of any sort, but she was for all for a romantic relationship by *ménage-a-trios* to fulfil Salome's desires for she'd hurt her.

The following day the Queen invited Salome to dinner, knowing she would play the mistress in *ménage-a-trios*. Salome sat opposite me and her feet touched my leg in a sensual motion and whispered: 'I love you.'

Vouch to save I came under Salome's spell, the wicked witch she was, succumbed to her temptation, having no self control. I whispered to my wife Salome had propositioned me and, lo and behold, a *ménage-a-trios* was about to unfold.

We went to bed, I in the middle, nestled two of the most beautiful women. Then it dawned on me what the archangel said about temptations. If I yielded to this, I'm sent to purgatory! If so, it is my own fault.

I looked at Grace. Her figure was divine, golden hair falling over her lily-white breasts. I glanced at stunning Salome, naked beside me, her body was beautiful like Nefertiti, the most beautiful women in the world. If Salome was to indulge in *ménage-a-trios* it would be the sign of corruption of the highest order - witchcraft in heaven!

It was like the Greek sailors, who were lured ashore by the beautiful sirens, dangerous women, shipwrecked on rocks if they yielded to the temptation. Sirens were not Aphrodite, the goddess of love, who would have saved the sailors. The sirens have sent the sailors to hell.

I turned away in disgust. I went to the lounge and took a drink, while the two women lusted into lesbianism.

Surely, it would not be allowed in paradise.

It's sacrilege!

I confronted Grace about her affair with Salome. She did not know what the fuss was about and said that I should take it as it comes.

'You said that we are friends, but why not be lovers?' said Grace, matter-of-factly. 'It happens.'

'All you want from Salome is *ménage-a-trios*. You forget we are married, union with body and soul, and you dismiss it,' I protested.

'Why don't you want to share love with me Salome?' asked Grace. 'Are you jealous that two women love each other?'

'You're bewitched!' I protested. 'Salome has a spell on you. She's evil and she lured you and me into a *ménage a trios*. She is a witch!'

'You'll regret that,' the Queen said. 'She is not a witch. Mark my words you will suffer the consequences.'

'I shall go to Our Lord and see what he says about your affair with Salome,' I said, protesting.

'If you do that the union of marriage will be over,' said the Queen, shaking her fist and stormed off with Salome.

Chapter 37

Adultery

I fled the Queen's palace and travelled to New Jerusalem to met Our Lord but he was away dealing with the Rapture ongoing since Armageddon. There to meet was the archangel Raphael.

I explained that I took his advice to marry the Queen and she took it upon herself to engage in *ménage-a-trios* with her lover Salome. 'What do you say about that? She has deceived me and the vows we took.'

'Salome is a loyal servant to Our Lady,' said the archangel. 'The Queen is not being unfaithful. She has a union with you and she is your wife. Adultery would be with another male. Queen is in love with you and Salome.'

'Is a *ménage-a-trios* is acceptable?' I said, aghast.

'Love is all that matters,' said Raphael. 'I must go now and prepare for the newcomers after the Rapture.'

I felt relieved that all that matters between women is love. I wanted to tell Grace and Salome that *ménage-a-trios* fine, but in moderation. However, something is wrong if I have an affair with Salome, for Grace is my wife and a soul partner, and I would be accused of adultery. I would have to talk with Grace and explain my predicament, for there is no peace unless it is settled.

On entering the palace I was told that Grace and Salome

have gone away to a secret cabin in the hillside to get away from the gossip and the city.

I rode with my stallion across the country to the place where they could only be, a valley hidden between the two mountains, south of New Jerusalem. I spotted a log cabin nestled in the trees about a mile away. There was smoke pouring out of the chimney and as I approached I saw Grace through the windows with Salome.

I went up to the door about to knock then curiosity overcame me. I looked again through the window, and Salome was going down on the Queen. Are the two women in love?

I quietly tip-toed to the bedroom there before me was Salome performing cunnilingus on Grace, every muscle in her body quivering until she reached orgasm and she cried out.

The orgasmic screaming was a turn on which affected me. I approached the two lovers, anticipating would respond to my request.

'How would you like to try out *ménage-a-trios*, in moderation?' I asked.

The Queen turned her head and kissed me on the lips, sealing our relationship with Salome and me in *ménage-a-trios*.

I made love to them both, insatiably.

That fateful night was my downfall.

Chapter 38

Celestial Court

I was summoned together with Salome to the High Celestial Court in New Jerusalem where archangel Michael sat with twelve angels. The archangel said that Our Lord and archangel Raphael were away in dealing with the Rapture and he was to sit in judgement on our *ménage-a-trios*.

'But the archangel Raphael told me that love is all that matters,' I said, protesting my innocence.

'You have sinned against God and heaven,' said St. Michael. 'Didn't you know there are three Spheres in Heaven? The first Sphere is the throne of the Almighty and archangels, the second is the angels and martyrs and third, the lowest, where all of the Christians are saved and there is hell. What say you to this charge?'

'I admit that I took part in *ménage-a-trios* but I pray in mitigation it was love,' I protested. 'It was love too,' said Salome, claiming her innocence.

'*Ménage-a-trios* are not love,' said St. Michael. 'It's sordid.'

The archangel and the twelve angels adjourned to discuss what sentence they would impose as I and Salome waited for that fatal day. In the afternoon they returned and offered their verdict - guilty!

'You and Salome have been exiled into purgatory until you repent of your sins,' announced archangel Michael.

'In the case of the Queen, there is no case against her. She is exonerated.'

'Can I see the Queen before I go?' I pleaded.

'Yes, and then go to purgatory where you belong,' said the St. Michael

I was escorted to the Queen's palace and said farewell to the only woman I truly loved, Grace. I looked around and there was no Salome to be seen.

'She's gone to purgatory and it's your fault,' said the Queen, enraged. 'Our union is over.'

With that I descended into the pains of purgatory.

Chapter 39

Darkness

On a dark night I entered into the gates of purgatory for the third time. The walls were black and I was descending into darkness at the speed of light until I reached the pit of suffering. And there was Salome!

'You are a witch'! I protested. 'You deceive me and the Queen by your treachery with *ménage-a-trios*. You're evil.'

Salome stood before me with a blood-curling snarl. 'You're the devil and that is why you've come to purgatory,' she said. 'You instigated *ménage-a-trios* when you came into the Queen's bedroom and seduced us, you philanderer.'

Her words pierced my heart. Salome was right. I'm a philanderer. That is why I'm here. 'Forgive me,' I confessed. 'I'm torn between the flesh and the spirit. I repent, forgive me. You're not a witch.'

I held out my hands, wanting to hold her. She paused not wanting to forgive me the way I have been accusing her and mistreating her. Then all of a sudden she yielded and threw her arms around me.

'Come with me,' I asked. 'There is light at the end of the tunnel.'

We held each other as we approached the end of the tunnel and there was a huge chasm in between the dark tunnel and the light.

'We can fly across,' I said, seeing the chasm below.

'We can't fly because we are in purgatory,' said Salome.

I forgot that in heaven I can fly, but now in purgatory the gift for flying is gone. 'Take the long route to the light and we can see where we are,' I said.

I held Salome arm and led her through an endless tunnel fill with huge snakes and demons crossing out path.

'I'm frightened,' said Salome.

'Stay close and all will be well,' I said, comforting her as we made our way through the dark tunnel of purgatory.

There were horrors that were beyond belief. Salome was tortured by severe violence which I couldn't prevent. She was raped by a hairy monster and it turned on me when I tried to rescue her. I fled and there is more agony when I entered the cave and walls closed in, almost suffocated me.

Salome caught up with me and we survived by the skin of our teeth and there before us were the open spaces and light all around us as we journey on towards the kingdom. I held her arm as we took our way to a secluded cave where we prayed for salvation and repentance.

In the cave I cried out for the archangel Raphael to come and restore me to heaven, but he could not hear me for the chasm between purgatory and heaven was too great.

I was left to suffer an endless of torrent of torture until eventually repentance came by the redeemed by the Blood of a Lamb.

Salome and I parted and I was called to a huge cathedral. There I was robed in a black habit, hood over my head, as I approached the altar and there was a shrunken head in a box nearby. I looked inside and fire poured down upon his head.

Could it be that one of the apostles received the Holy Spirit by fire rained upon his head? A voice told me that I could move his head until the fire was right over his skull. I stepped back and looked at the fire coming down, almost like a bishop's mitre. He was indeed an apostle.

I retreated from the altar and a priest walks by and me calls me 'Fr. Gregory,' the name of the Superior Father, who inducted to into the community of monks in the monastery on earth.

Then a huge gathering of tourists passed in front of me as I stepped aside and wondering what I was doing there. Who is the apostle with the severed head in the box?

The black habit given to me by the Benedictine's Order was a reminder of the dark night I went through the gates of purgatory. It's the traumatic experience of St. John of the Cross in the Dark Night of the Soul all those years ago. He recalled those dark nights of purging his soul through intense contemplation to Divine Wisdom, Love of God.

Maybe head in the box was St. John, veneration of his sainthood. Maybe God is calling me to be a saint?

That is why I longed for freedom like St. John of the Cross, purging his soul of all distractions to become a saint. But I'm weary and I would humbly take the mercy of God to get to heaven, a poor sinner that I am. That would be my penance, hoping to attain my freedom in paradise.

Now I am here in purgatory I have nothing to rely on save God, for the archangels, including my devoted Raphael, have abandoned me. My only salvation is to pray to Our Lord.

In the meantime, where is Salome? I have looked in caves and forests until I found her weeping outside a cabin. 'What is the matter?' I ask, concerned.

'I have been in *ménage-a-trios*,' said Salome. 'I have sinned.'

'I know,' I said.

'No, there's another sin!' exclaimed Salome. 'I have met a priest who shamed me. I was in the cabin and the priest and the young woman came to stay and he forced to have *ménage-a-trios.*'

'Why did you do it?'

'The priest forced me,' said Salome, crying, 'he's so strong.'

'We all need to go for confession,' I said, resignedly. 'You must get up and follow me to the cathedral where all is forgiven, like St Magdalene who was a prostitute.

We made our way to the cathedral and made our confession. I blurted out my sins and Salome confessed she was the instigator of the first *ménage-a-trios* and not the second time. She was forced to take part. She knelt in the chapel and I took the staircase down into the cathedral basement, the crypt, and looked at the replicas of saints now in heaven.

There in the corner was a replica of St. John of the Cross. I looked at the replica and on it said: 'It's love alone makes the heart long for beloved. It moves and guide and makes it to soars upward to God. Now happy is the night.'

At last I have been redeemed and knowing that I am bound to heaven for St. John of the Cross knows my heart all is forgiven. I raced up the steps and found Salome weeping at the foot of the Cross.

'All is forgiven,' I said, excitedly. 'Now, we will go to heaven.'

Chapter 40

Lowest in Heaven

Salome and I entered heaven with a fanfare of angels playing their trumpets. We were paraded through New Jerusalem on unicorns and the crowds were singing Alleluias, Alleluias, but the fanfare didn't last.

We were escorted to the archangels office and be assigned the lowest places in heaven. Salome was to wash-up the dishes and I swept kitchen floor and cleaning out the toilets. We are given the jobs on Sphere 3 because that is lowest place in heaven. We are not as yet pure, hence the toilets and washing-up the lowest duties.

It was humiliation to teach us humility in the face of obstacles, namely cleaning out the loos, like 'jankers' in the forces for punishment. We toiled for about a month when we were called the office and gave us another job - feeding the Christians who had fled through Rapture.

Salome, who had maternal instincts in abundance, diligently fed the hungry. Some Christians didn't want a meal because they felt purified. The same thing goes for the Jews as they were also purified by the blood of Christ.

Salome in her zest at feeding the hungry was promoted to the Sphere 2 where she waited on the angels. My position as Director of the Divine Crusaders was reinstated as the crusaders were about to fend off the enemy at the border in the eastern hemisphere.

I rode on my stallion for the palace and was about to recall Divine Crusaders when the Queen appeared. 'I want to see you,' she said.

'I am truly sorry. You weren't at fault over Salome. I want to make it up to you before you go with the Divine Crusaders.'

'But you said the union was over?'

'That was then, this is now,' stated the Queen. 'Come to my boudoir.'

I had to do what the Queen wanted. We made love that afternoon and it was divine and reconciled us.

I called the Divine Crusaders and we set off to annihilate the demons in an attempt to usurp the Kingdom.

The demons were led by the Amazon warrior Scarlet with two legions who invaded by the north border. It was like Armageddon. The Divine Crusaders attacked with the Holy Spirit and Scarlet and the legions fell into the fire and brimstone which hell provided.

The Divine Crusaders returned to my palace and we had triumphal feast, bringing in the dancing girls from the east, and drinking wine.

The next morning I was called to New Jerusalem and was told by the archangels, in view of my excellent battle on the eastern hemisphere, I have been promoted to Sphere 2.

I was escorted by St. Raphael to the parade ground as Seraphic and Cherub put golden wings on my back infused by the Holy Spirit.

I was taken up by the archangels and triumphantly announced that I was an angel with spiritual powers even a Pope would envy. Solomon had achieved wisdom but with the powers I had been given I could see in the past and in the future.

And so it happens, the spiritual birth by sexual intercourse, which I'd denied was for an archangel was born on a spiritual planet, which the archangels were gathered around a crib.

I said to an angel: 'I don't believe it. There isn't any births in heaven, is there?'

The angel looked at me. 'There is another planet higher than heaven where the archangels gave birth, the spiritual home of the Almighty.'

'I am told that His throne was in New Jerusalem?' I said, confuse.

'There is another planet where the Lord is enthroned, the pinnacle of paradise,' said the angel.

'Can I go there?' I asked, eagerly.

'No, because you're not an archangel,' he said, and went off to praise God.

I looked and saw the other spiritual planets circling round the Almighty planet. There was no sun but an eternal light shone forth throughout paradise. The light came within the spiritual planets and reached the hearts of everyone, including me.

I look over my shoulders at the golden wings and thought how blessed I was to be an angel. My sexual urges were gone and like an angel I was asexual. I had no thoughts of romancing the Queen and no more affection for my ex-wives. I was heading for enlightenment and a pure heart.

I thought of my mother and out of compassion Salome. My mother was now in heaven attending the hungry after the Rapture along with Salome. Sarah was with them but the other wife Sherma was in purgatory. Of all the powers I had as an angel, I could not help her because of her spiritual journey was predestined. She struggled to get out of Buddha-land, where the souls are ever reincarnated, to be with Christ.

Salome was doing all right. She was promoted to running the Jews' sports and music centre in the heart of New Jerusalem, renowned for heavenly choral music and sport activities.

My destination was to reach out for the spiritual planets. There were a dozen around the Almighty planet and numerous spiritual planets as far as the eye could see. It was infinite paradise.

I was to lead the legion of angels to explore numerous spiritual planets and to colonise them for Christians saved by the Rapture. I and the legion of angels set about arranging new homes in heaven for Christians after the Rapture. They were thrilled at seeing paradise and a new earth.

I prioritise new homes for Christians into twelve planets close to the Almighty planet and later for the newcomers' homes in spiritual planets way beyond into paradise. There were countless spiritual planets, far more than we could imagine. Jesus said that 'many rooms in heaven' for Christians in the afterlife.

The angels divided the new Christians into sections and led them to the twelve spiritual planets and their eternal homes. People from Europe, Asia, Africa, U.S., Australia, the Middle East and South America had arrived. The Christians were pure in heart having gone through the Rapture. They were not separated but all mixed with other people from different countries, like Jesus said.

I was appointed the head of the Heavenly Twelve Planets serving God the Almighty, a Golden Star enthroned with Our Lord. All the Christians on the twelve planets served God day and night and pronounced him Emanuel, God is with us.

My duty is to visit each of the planets and to improve the worship with all its fanfare and triumphs resonating though out the heavens. My first port of call was to attend the Venus, the planet close to the Golden Star.

I was greeted by the Queen of Venus, a relative of Queen Victoria. She was divine, her blue hair matched the robe and her eyes sparkled green. I was presented to the Queen by angels. Some of the angels touched my wings and said what magnificent gold wings they were.

'We are white wings because we don't have enough purity,' said one of the angels.

'We shall get golden wings one day,' the other angel said.

I turned to Queen Venus and asked her if Queen Victoria, her cousin, made it through to heaven. I know, of course, I can see in the future but I want to hear from here.

'She's on another planet,' said the Queen. 'She's well.'

'What's the name of the planet and I can visit her?' I asked, hopefully.

'Utopia,' said Queen Venus. 'Send her my regards.'

'Utopia, that's the name of a perfect planet,' I said. 'I shall visit you again soon. Farewell my Queen Venus.'

I met with the Divine Crusaders. They visited four planets and all was well but they had not visited Utopia.

I combed my golden wings and set out to meet Queen Victoria and her husband, Prince Albert.

There was a regal welcome when I flew into Queen Victoria's palace. The triumphant fanfare greeted me and the Divine Crusaders, who entered the court with unicorns.

There were dancing girls who were dressed in scanty outfits

with their arms waving at the crusaders. In the palace we were introduced to a delighted Queen Victoria. On earth she went through forty years of being a widow, and now she was eternally with her husband, whom she loved all those years.

I sat down on the couch and a bikini girl offered an apricot brandy and another girl offered a foot massage. I was surprised at the lavish entertainment because Queen Victoria had mourned the loss of her husband for all those years. Now in the company of Prince Albert she was fulfilled as a woman and free at last for entertainment.

The Divine Crusaders were enjoying themselves with the girls and their frolics and the apricot brandy. All was well until a messenger told me that the border and had been breached by demons.

Chapter 41

War in Heaven

War is declared on the outskirts of heaven, the archangels announced. I said farewell to Queen Victoria then rounded up the twelve Divine Crusaders and ordered them to battle.

It was the north-eastern hemisphere that demons were invading the border and there was Scarlet, the Amazon warrior, who led the charge hurling over the border with ten thousand devils about to usurp heaven.

I and the Divine Crusaders repelled them at about a mile over the border and the demons retreated. Only a few demons who had crossed the river hurled themselves at the crusaders. I intervened and I held out the crucifixion in my hand. I called upon the Holy Spirit exorcise the invaders. There was a rush when the Holy Spirit stuck and the demons fell down into the furnace.

There was one of them saved, their leader Scarlet. She stood before me, breathing fire from her mouth and a sword in her hands. I struck her down with a blow and tied both hands and feet and carried into my palace.

There before was the devil incarnate, Scarlet, as I tied her to the pillar and confronted her. 'Why has Satan invaded heaven?' I asked.

'I told you before, Satan wants the Kingdom of Heaven,' said Scarlet, her eyes filled with rage.

'You will never let foot in heaven, do you hear me,' I remonstrated, 'nor the demons nor Lucifer.'

'You do not know my powers,' Scarlet said, breaking the chain to the pillar.

'You do not know the power of the Holy Spirit!' I said, breathing down the Holy Spirit on her. All of a sudden Scarlet fell beneath my feet like a quivering girl, yielding to the Holy Spirit with her arms outstretched and crying:

'I yield,' Scarlet said, 'do with me as you want.'

'Now you have come to your senses,' I said, 'I will show you what's to come in paradise, if you repent?'

'I do repent of all my sins,' she confessed.

I took Scarlet to a waterfall and there the colours of the rainbow were falling like the stars enhancing the whole of the universe. Like a child in a magic shop, Scarlet was overcome by the immensity of it all.

'It's magical,' said Scarlet, 'now that I've known coming to heaven, it's wonderful.'

'If you want we can go on a magical ride,' I said, taking the four unicorns and hitching them up to a sulky. 'Hop aboard I'll take on a magical trip.'

I looked at Scarlet. She was transformed by the Holy Spirit. Her dark eyes were set alight by golden eyes that sparkle when I looked at her.

We took off to a remote cabin by the lake. It was here that I was overcome by Scarlet's change. She changed from Amazon warrior into a child of God, not wanting to be overbearing, but subdued by the Holy Spirit, like the Mother of God.

'You have you denounced the devil?' I asked, apprehensively.

'Yes, I have,' Scarlet said, earnestly.

'If you have truly confessed, you are forgiven,' I said. 'That's how it is in heaven.'

'I truly confess,' said Scarlet, falling into my arms. She lay there with an angelic smile that captured my heart.

From that day on I was in love with her.

Chapter 42

In Love with Scarlet

The archangels were meeting in New Jerusalem with a new agenda. On top of the list was my involvement with Scarlet. One of the angels told them that I was in love with Scarlet after she invaded heaven.

'She's a devil,' the angel said. 'She led the demons over the border trying to invade us. She is an Amazon warrior with legions of demons and they were destroyed, but Scarlet was taken prisoner by the chief of the Divine Crusaders and he fell in love with her!'

Archangel Michael said my love with Scarlet were treason, tore his garment in two, and turned to St. Raphael. 'You have led him from purgatory and tutored him. Why he has done this? He is in with the Scarlet, the devil. Go and see him and tell him to come to New Jerusalem and answer these charges.'

Archangel Raphael stood up and said he was not aware of these charges. 'I shall go and see him and bring him back here.' With that he left the synod and flew back to the eastern hemisphere, but I was not there.

I and Scarlet took a boat to a remote island that was surreal. It was a heavenly home, far from the bustle of New Jerusalem, with its palm beaches and sandy coves. We put on our swimsuits, mine a blue shorts and hers a pink bikini and we had a swim.

But I had forgotten my duties as the chief of the Divine Crusaders, as lay down on the sandy beach. Scarlet noticed something in the bush and we approached with caution and lo and behold it was a fairy.

'It's extraordinary,' I exclaimed. 'It was started in Ireland with a myth. There were lots of fairies in the gardens.'

With that there were fairies surrounding us, different colours, red, white, blue and gold and love all around us. We were one in paradise.

'I feel like making love to you,' said Scarlet, lying in the sand next to me.

Scarlet opened her lips and kissed me, a tingling feeling inside like I've never felt before. I felt her warm body, her magnificent breasts there to be fondled. She parted her legs and surrendered, yielding to my inner most desire to be one with Scarlet, a converted warrior into a child of God.

But it was not meant to be. For out of the blue like a thunder ball there was archangel Raphael brandishing his wings like fury.

'I've come a long way to trace you and Scarlet,' said the archangel. 'You are summoned to attend the court in New Jerusalem.'

'But what for?' I asked. 'We're on a romantic holiday!'

'You will find out in due course,' said St. Raphael.

'You're not telling me?'

'No, I've been kind to you before, but not this time,' said St. Raphael, abruptly. 'I shall see you in Jerusalem. Farewell.'

I looked at Scarlet. 'There's something wrong,' I said.

We hurried back to New Jerusalem to know our fate.

Chapter 43

Treason

At the Court of New Jerusalem I and Scarlet were charged with treason. We were summoned with our hands and feet bound.

Archangel Michael, prosecuting, said that in view of the serious of the charge, I was brought down to the level Sphere 3, where some of the Christians were impure. The Lord had the power on level 3 to evict those whose deeds were impure to purgatory and even hell.

St. Michael outlined the case. He said Scarlet and I, by falling in love, conspired to overthrow the kingdom with treason. 'Scarlet was the instigator. She was the devil's advocate, an Amazon warrior, who led the legions of demons to invade the heaven.

'They were found on the Love Island where they fell in love and Scarlet bewitched him to form an alliance against Our Lord by attempting usurp his kingdom. The witness to that effect was the archangel Raphael, who caught them in the act of making love,' said St. Michael. 'I call St. Raphael to the witness box.'

I looked across to where Scarlet standing. She was adamant and defiant as the prosecution said there ample evidence against her. She was in love with me and 'hell or high water' could separate us.

'You recall them making love when you arrived?' asked the prosecution.

'They said they're on a romantic holiday,' said the archangel Raphael.

'Were they in love?' asked St. Michael.

'Indeed, they were,' answered the archangel.

'Yes, that's true,' I said from the dock.

St. Michael said there were no further questions. 'You have heard it from his own mouth that he was in love with her and conspired to overthrow the kingdom.'

I was called to the stand. 'I and Scarlet were in love. She was a new woman, converted by the Holy Spirit,' I said, with conviction. 'I cast out demons in her by exorcism. Scarlet is a new Christian and serves the Lord.'

'I'm a humble servant,' Scarlet repeated.

'Welcome to my kingdom,' said Our Lord, presiding. 'You are free.'

With that the guards unchained us to begin our new life with God, forgiving all those who brought to charges.

With Scarlet we can visit the planets surrounding God's kingdom and secure the borders with our faithful crusaders.

Chapter 44

The Golden Star

Twelve spiritual planets circled around the Golden Star, which is God's throne. Having visited a few planets, namely Queen Victoria's Utopia and the planet of Queen Venus, I set sail on the quest for the other planets.

The first was the majestic planet Mars 2 unlike the original Mars with its red atmosphere and hostile environment it had a vibrant and friendly welcome when we arrived. There to greet me were the Saints of the past now resurrected to a new life with God. They were called Saints Eternal and they led me to new city, named Holy Saints, and showered me with garlands.

The Saints showed me the part of the city where the contemplative nuns stayed with their Benedictine habits and white veils. Scarlet went to the convent for two weeks on retreat and said on returning: 'I want to join them, contrition for the sins I have caused.'

'It's a contemplative order,' I remarked. 'You don't want to make love anymore?' I asked.

'It's God wish,' Scarlet said, kissing on my lips for one last time. 'God bless you.' With that she entered the convent.

About six months had passed when I asked the Mother Superior how Scarlet was and she said that she was a novice nun and professed to a contemplative nun in the community.

I asked if I could see Scarlet but the Mother Superior told

me that she had taken the vow of a contemplative nun and was forbidden to entertain guests.

God works miracles.

Chapter 45

A thousand years

All Christians from the 12 planets were thrilled when the archangels announced there was a month celebrations and festival for the King of the Universe, Our Lord. They were called to the God's Star, rejoicing and praising Our Lord. All bowed to worship Him and they sang Alleluias as they circled to the throne of the Almighty celebrating the feast of Our Lord and Paradise, our true home.

Excused from the gatherings were the contemplative nuns. I could never see Scarlet again, although at the gathering I looked out for her to no avail. She was holding a vigil at the convent for the Rapture.

There were legion of angels dancing round the throne and the seraphim and cherub were holding their hands up in worship to their Lord. The archangels and the Mother of God were there sitting beside Our Lord. Then from far and wide, winged angels and trumpets hailed the dawn of new age in heaven.

Then the Lord stood up and sadly announced to the stadium that he was going away.

'Where too?' the archangels asked.

'I am going back to the new Earth to set up my throne and hence it will be a thousand years of peace, a new millennium,' said the Lord.

'Can we can come to?' asked the archangel Gabriel.

'No,' said the Lord. 'I shall take the Director of the Divine Crusaders. He will lead my mission and announce my presence with legions of angels.'

I was called before the Lord and he blessed all Christians for what turns out for a mission peace that will endure for a thousand years.

Our Lord gathered the legions of angels to visit the new earth, ten times larger than the original earth, wiped out by the sun and nuclear bombs.

Our Lord and the angels sounding their trumpets announced to the heavens a New Earth full of spiritual power, peace and love. He was to sit on the throne and destroyed Satan to establish new home for all Christians.

Our Lord called the 12 tribes of Israel to sit on his throne and judge Christians who are worthy to enter paradise. All the Christian were taken to be judged, but others, who abused children, await justice.

Before the court were priests from all countries like America, Australia, England and Germany facing sexual abuses, several of them carried out for many years. All the clergy, except those who repented at the last moment, were thrown into hell of eternal torment.

Now all Christians who repented were free to enter the New Earth for a thousand years. The legion of angels with their trumpets blowing as I entered the green and pleasant land of the New Earth.

There were no cities or towns but the New Earth was full of worshippers flocking to see Our Lord, Jesus Christ, from all parts of the globe, to the east and west, from the north to the south, all praising Our Maker.

They sang: 'Alleluias, Alleluias, Alleluias.'
All was peace - for the time being!

Chapter 46

Soul mate

All the archangels were gathered around the altar. I asked St. Raphael what is the requirements for being an archangel, now I've promoted to an angel.

If I were an archangel I would be welcomed in Sphere 1 where the Lord is enthroned. In addition there would be sexual relations between archangels producing offspring. They are allowed have sex, being holy pure.

Archangel Raphael said that if I was called to be an archangel heaven he would rejoice. 'Look what you have done in securing borders and defied demons but you must first go before the Lord to become an archangel.

'It's God will can I have a female archangel for a soul mate, just like I had on earth?' I asked, hopefully.

'You have anything you want as an archangel, but the Lord is happy being asexual, for celibacy is a higher calling,' said St. Raphael.

'You don't want women, is that it?' I asked.

'I love women, but being asexual is what Jesus wants.'

The archangels stood up, feathered their wings, St Raphael blessed me, and they flew away.

It is a higher calling but is up to an archangel to chose what if he wants a bride or not. It is his prerogative.

I will seek a soul mate and I go to Our Lord for his permission to be promoted to an archangel.

In the wilderness I prayed for God's will. If it is God's will for me to be an archangel I will take up the responsibility with most humble endeavours and find a soul mate.

There on the mountain I prayed for three whole days and night, not eating nor drinking. It is the most intense prayer and I was truly humbled and wept for I was ready to go before the Lord to seek his will.

Chapter 47

A Suitor

I was called to Our Lord in the highest planet, the Golden Star, on which the Almighty sat on his heavenly throne. I kneeled before him and gave the sign of the cross.

'I'm here before you, Our Lord, to petition you to send me the Sphere 1 to attend your needs with the archangels. I defended your kingdom from demons and I was promoted as an angel and now let me be one of your archangels in paradise,' I implored.

Our Lord said: 'I will accept your petition that you will become an archangel but I've heard from the archangels that you denounce chastity in favour of an archangel wife. Why is that?'

'I am not perfect my Our Lord, but with my soul mate I shall become one,' I said, with humility.

'Let it be said, you have my permission to enter my kingdom as an archangel,' said the Lord. 'Go out to the universe and with your partner and multiply. Do you have an archangel partner in mind?'

'No my Lord,' I said, 'but I shall find one.'

'Blessings upon you,' said the Lord.

With that I departed, bowing to Our Lord, and hoping that in the next weeks I shall find my soul mate and marry her eternally.

Chapter 48

Planet Cupid

Among the spiritual planets, the most romantic by female archangels is planet Cupid. It is one of the twelve planets who circled the Gold Star of which Our Lord is worshipped.

I arrived on Cupid and was adored by servants, who were there to serve the virgins archangels looking for their husbands. I was about to meet them. Other archangels were married after a romantic affair, hence Cupid, giving its name.

I was invited to my first female archangel. She lived in the palace not far from the city, Eros. A servant introduced me to the archangel, her face was golden with blue eyes and long blonde hanging down her waist and she wore a white gown with a diamond necklace. She looked stunning.

'I'm delighted,' she said, 'I'm Helena, the archangel looking for love. Do sit down. Have you come far?'

'I've come from Our Lord to make a journey of romance. Will you come for a dinner tonight?' I asked, hopefully.

'Yes, but we have the dinner served here by servants,' said Helena. 'Don't worry the food is not poisonous, but rather aphrodisiac.'

'Yes, I bet.'

'Do have a drink,' said Helena. She rang the bell and a servant came out with a wine list. She passed it to me.

'I'll have a cognac,' ignoring the wine. 'It exhilarates me.'

'I'll have the same,' said Helena.

We sipped our cognacs and the soft music and the dim lights played on my romantic thoughts as I watched Helena finished her drink.

Her smile and blonde hair made me come closer and I smelt the aroma of perfume filled the air, rose I think. I held her hand and I was about to say a poem I wrote when all of a sudden she kissed me. I stared into her crystal blue eyes, her face was radiant like a goddess and we embrace like lovers.

We went to bed that night as soul mates.

I found my perfect archangel.

Chapter 49

A New Wife

The sun glistened like a shining star as the spiritual planets circled round in heaven. With my new wife archangel Helena we travelled through the cosmos to visit New Earth. It was a new experience for her, not having been there.

Thousands of Christians were going to the mountain to celebrate Jesus return and restore paradise. We joined them in their pilgrimage and sang Alleluias, Alleluias.

On reaching the summit before Jesus came the elders built one large tent from which the service began. With my wife we were presented to the crowd.

Then Jesus appeared from the clouds: 'Peace be upon you. You have inherited a thousand years of peace and you will be heralded throughout heaven.'

Then the crowd formed a line and received a blessing from the Lord, bowing on their hands and knees in humility, saying 'Emanuel, Emanuel, God is with us.'

I and Helena stood beside Our Lord, one on the left and the right, as the crowd was blessed. After the blessings the Lord turned to Helena. 'Blessing is upon you as your husband. You shall give birth and multiply.'

With that Our Lord took off over the clouds.

I looked at Helena. She was radiantly beautiful her archangel golden wings looked majestic. We departed with our blessings and said goodbye to the crowd on our way to planet Cupid.

It was there that we conceived an offspring because the archangels would not be allowed to have sexual relations other than Cupid. For it was here that the archangels would make love on honeymoon.

We arrived at Cupid at the most auspicious time, for love was flourishing. It was a spring time. I took Helena to a cove where the archangels made love and placed her gently on her bed and snuggled up to her, brushing her golden wings aside. Her arms entwined with mine and I felt oneness with her as I entered her with the spiritual love divine.

A few weeks later she told me that she was pregnant.

My heart was joyful and we celebrated the news. What it is a boy or female archangel? I said it's a boy we called him Adam and if it's a girl we called her Princess.

So came the time when Helena goes into labour, not the nine months which we had on the earth, but she delivered the female archangel in three months without maternal suffering.

Now our daughter is born. Joy was beaming from Helena as she cuddled her baby. It was a happy experience until one day something happened and Helena and I were devastated.

Our Princess sitting in her cot when her wings caught in the frame and no matter how she managed to free herself the wings asphyxiated her.

Helena was inconsolable.

All it not well in paradise. Accidents do happen.

We buried Princess, our joy and happiness. A legion of archangels attended the service and our Princess was laid to rest at Paradise Cemetery.

Princess died knowing that the spiritual bodies were eternal, for so it seems. We prayed about it and nothing happened until St. Michael told me that our baby died of a curse. That curse came from witchcraft.

It's inconceivable that witchcraft would enter heaven again. I was to find out later from where the curse had from.

Chapter 50

Grief over Princess

Helena and I grieved and no matter how we longed for our Princess to return she wasn't coming back. I set about who was to blame for her death.

Scarlet was not was not to blame for she was converted and now she is a consecrated nun. That leaves Salome! She was last seen as head of the Jewish music and sports centre.

Salome was infiltrating witchcraft in the Jewish centre which holds about 1,000 students. Heaven would be afflicted because of the Salome curse. That would explain why our beloved Princess had died.

I would seek out Salome and know the truth. Is she a witch or not!

I arrived at the centre and I asked the receptionist if Salome was in the building.

'No, she hasn't been here for the past three months,' said the receptionist. 'I don't know where she went and she didn't leave a message.'

With that I entered the building and looked for a student she was tutoring. I came across a spotty teenager who said she went out one night and never came back.

'Where was she going,' I asked.

'To a meeting,' the teenager said. 'I don't know where the meeting was held.'

'Who organised the meeting?'

'Salome said it was a secret meeting, that's all.'

I thanked the teenager and set about finding what the secret meeting is for and where it was held. I dread to think it was a black coven and Salome was a wizard. How would a wizard enter heaven?

Jesus said the devil knows no bounds and turns darkness into light and light into darkness.

On venturing out where the meeting is held I passed by the Avenue of Worshippers and there was a hall at the far end of the avenue and it had name on the top of the building which read: 'Black Mass at Midnight'.

On going in I saw witches holding a service where a priest held out her hand and blessed the congregation. It was Salome, a wizard.

Salome was ordained after she left the centre by members of the coven. She is a priest of the witches and I stood there devastated. I stood at the back where I could not be seen and hurriedly slid out of the back door. If I confronted Salome the whole coven would have attacked me.

I made hasty retreat along the avenue and back to home where I sought refuge from Our Lord. He knows what to do. I prayed about all night long but then the Holy Spirit told me to round up the Divine Crusaders and destroy the coven and send Salome into hell where she belongs.

Chapter 51

Spiritual Victory

I rounded up twelve Crusaders and told them what was in store for them. A coven of witches led by Salome invaded parts of heaven and wants to usurp the Kingdom.

'You must destroy them,' I said, urgently. 'You must go in and cast down all of them into the eternal fire. Go with God and I will show where they are.'

I led the Crusaders with shield and sword to defend the faith and restore paradise to its rightful place in the universe. We invaded the coven and the witches about to celebrate a Black Mass at midnight.

There were about a hundred of witches praying invoking the spirit of Satan to appear before them. I burst in and confronted Salome as the Crusaders attempted to cast witches into everlasting hell.

There was pandemonium breaking out in the hall as the coven of witches led by Salome attacks the Crusaders. Battles were going on for an hour when Salome and the witches were beaten by the fierce onslaught of the Crusaders amounting to eighty witches died at the scene.

Salome stood before the corpses and said: 'No more. The witches have been defeated by the Holy Spirit.'

Salome and the other witches were paraded before me and the crusaders about to hear the sentence.

'You will go henceforth to hell where fire will burn you for eternity,' I said. 'Salome will be the first.'

The Divine Crusaders took them to the border and threw them into the eternal fire which they were burned for a thousand years and more.

Chapter 52

Rejoice

On returning to New Jerusalem I told the archangels that Salome and the witches were defeated. I said there was a fierce battle and eighty witches were killed. Salome was the first to go into hell followed by the witches. She confessed the coven was about to take over the kingdom.

'Well done,' said the archangel Michael. 'You sent the witches to hell.'

'Not my doing,' I interceded, 'but the Holy Spirit. But why were the eighty witches died in battle when they were in the state of heaven where no-one dies because they were in spiritual bodies?'

Archangel Gabriel said: 'Those who infiltrated heaven deceived the word of God by robbing themselves with Christian white robes. They weren't spiritual. You found them out and cast into hell. You deserve reward in heaven.'

I was honoured by archangels but at the thought of Salome of bewitching me that she was in a nun and about to overthrow the kingdom by witchcraft was unspeakable. Salome deserves her punishment, not forgetting our daughter's death. Her witchcraft was all down to her mother, hanged in Salem with the other witches.

My spiritual journey goes on with no more invasions shown by the coven of witches. Now is the time to dance for joy in paradise. Now is the time for rejoicing.

Chapter 53

Faith, Hope and Love

My wife Helena introduced to three virgins, Faith, Hope and Love, archangels living nearby. Helena did not want children, so upset by losing Princess.

She wanted me to explore the possibility of having a baby with one of the virgins, for jealousy and possessiveness were not part of her life.

'Now go and meet them for they are the most beautiful and intelligent women you'll ever meet,' remarked Helena, showing me where they lived.

'Aren't you coming?' I asked. 'You invited me?'

'Don't be silly,' Helena said. 'I'm not a jealous type. Now go and have fun.'

With that I made my way to the house they shared on Mount Avenue and knocked on the door. Hope answered the door and was pleased to see me. She fluttered her wings joyfully and led me into the lounge where I met her housemates, Faith and Love.

I was struck by the stunning beauty of them all, every figure and every face were divine. I looked at every one of them, memorizing by their innate beauty. I ask everyone to tell me about their lives, starting with Hope.

She had only been an archangel for a short time, having been consecrated with golden wings by Our Lord.

'Before, I was an angel carrying souls to heaven, who have escaped the Rapture. It was heaven taking to their new home in eternity,' said Hope, gleefully.

'Before being angel did you come from Earth,' I said, queried.

'Oh no!' she said, 'I was born an angel.'

I turned to Faith sitting by the fire. There was an holy aura around her as she spoke about her faith in Our Lord.

'I too have rescued souls from the earth and brought them to heaven, she said, flapping her wings. I noticed with Faith there was a calm voice when she spoke with a tone so mellow it soothed the heart. I asked Faith we could go for a walk, to listen to her story of what paradise has done for her.

We walked by the river as she explained what it is for her being a relatively new archangel. 'It was being transported into a new life. We have responsibility here but we are free to do what we want,' said Faith, gleefully.

'Do you want to have children? I asked hopefully.

'We don't have children,' she admonished. 'We have arch-angel babies.'

'That's what I come about,' I said. 'We can have a baby archangel together?'

'Is not like that,' she said, protesting. 'Let us know each other and then we can talk about having an offspring.'

'It's like that on earth,' I said, despondently. 'Why can't we just make love?'

'Love all that matters,' said Faith. 'Love is universal and eternal. Have you been on the Holy Way, you know, transporting souls from earth to heaven?'

'No, I haven't.'

'Come, I just received a message to transport souls and you

as an archangel should come. I shall lead the way,' said Faith.

'The Bible says that the angels transport souls not the arch-angels,' I said.

'That's true but the archangels have the responsibility to ensure that Christian VIP's brought into the heaven safely,' answered Faith.

'What is Christian VIP's?' I said, hesitatingly.

'They are martyrs of the faith. The archangels comfort them on the heavenly way, as in Holy Way,' said Faith, with conviction.

'I shall come with you,' I said. 'It is a real blessing.' We spread our wings and flew up in to the clouds away from Paradise towards the scorched earth. There were thousands of souls waiting to be taken to heaven.

'Where shall we start?' I asked, 'There are so many of them.'

'We shall take the VIP's then the rest will be taken up by the Rapture to heaven by legions of angels,' said Faith.

'Where do we find the martyrs?' I asked, perplexed.

'Come, and I'll show you,' said Faith and took me to where the sun was scorching the earth in the region of North America.

'Why North America,' I asked, 'did they do something wrong?'

'Why yes,' said Faith. 'They put their faith in materialism not God. They burnt up a whole country by greed. There are few to be saved and we shall take them up to heaven as martyrs.'

'I haven't been on the Holy Way before,' I said, unfortunately.

'What were you before you became an archangel?' said Faith.

'I was born in England and angel took me heaven. From there I spent awhile in purgatory and then I was promoted in heaven and became an angel and then an archangel,' I said.

'Now we shall go to the Valley of the Dolls where we shall see the martyrs shedding their blood for their faith, awaiting their souls to be taken by you and me to heaven,' said Faith. 'Let us go and deliver them.'

We swooped down into the valley and rounded up the martyrs one by one and carried them back to their homeland, paradise.

It was so fitting. The martyrs' souls were transported to heaven with a spiritual body that will last forever.

Chapter 54

Hope

On going back home Faith introduce me to Hope, the second virgin archangel I was about to be dating. Hope had one ambition.

'I want to become a Super-Archangel,' she said.

'What's that?' I asked.

'I want to branch out across the universe with such power even God would be amazed,' said Hope.

'What, you're not going be one with God,' I asked, perplexed. 'That's Satan wants.'

'Oh no silly,' said Hope. 'I want to serve with the utmost will and I hope to be an archangel worthy of the highest calling. I want to be an archangel diva.'

'What would you change?'

'For a start, we speak the same language,' said Hope. 'All of the people who come from Earth speak different languages.'

'Aramaic?' I said, the language Jesus used on Earth.

'No, we are in heaven,' said Hope. 'We should all speak from the Holy Spirit.'

'What language is that?'

'Divine language,' answered Hope.

'How would you introduce that?

'With prayer,' answered Hope, with honesty.

With that we spread our wings and flew over the river as we

made our way to the Holy Mountain, majestic on the east coast of heaven. There was a festival for all the newly Christians who have reached heaven by Rapture.

Archangel Hope is presenting the awards, an eternal gold watch to all Christians who had gathered there at the foot of the mountain. 'You can see the eyes of Christians so happy by their salvation,' said Hope, presenting the awards.

After the rewards all Christians were sent to a dispersal unit. From there each was one was given a house in which they could live temporarily until a permanent home was made available, repeating the housing shortage on earth because of the huge influx of Christians by way of Rapture.

Hope and I flew home and we were greeted by Faith and Love. The two archangels said they were thrilled by Hope presenting the rewards and the three embraced one another.

'There were lots of Christians there. We gave every Christian an eternal watch save one whom had his arms been blown off by the explosion,' said Hope. 'He was transformed later in a spiritual body with new arms.'

Chapter 55

Love

Archangel Love came up to me and said: 'You have not asked me out on a date. Have you not forgotten me?'

'On the contrary,' I said. 'Love is all that matters to me. That's why I have asked you for a date last of all. Will you come on a love voyage with me?'

Archangel Love spread her wings with joy and said: 'I would love too.'

With that I bade farewell to archangels Faith and Hope and flew archangel Love to the remote island of Cupid where archangels fall in love.

It was paradise. Sandy beaches and palm trees for miles stretched along the coast where dolphins dance to waves. At the far end of the island there was a hut and we sauntered along the beach holding hands.

On reaching the beach hut we went inside and in the corner was a bed with pillows and a chest of drawers. On seeing the bed archangel Love went over and lay upon it, spreading her divine body. I looked across at her, stretching out her wings and beckoning me to come over.

'Come here and kiss me,' said archangel Love, 'and I will give you love.'

'You want to make love?' I asked, excited.

'Come here and I'll show you love,' said Love, teasing.

'Making love, I'll get you pregnant,' I said. 'That's what you want?'

Love spread out her wings around me. I was submitting to all her needs, beginning with love.

'That's what you want is love then your seed into me and I will make an archangel baby. Make love to me,' she begged. 'Take me.'

I look down on her divine body all spread out like a divine virgin wanting to take her virginity. Love clutched me as I went down on her holding her wings. She held me tight as I entered her. The wings fell limp as she lay there in throws of ecstasy and she arched her back and cried out in orgasmic bliss. All of her muscles shuddered as I came inside her.

She lay on the bed blissfully happy, but exhausted.

'Your seed was inside of me now,' said Love. 'We are part of one another - and more so if I'm pregnant!'

'You're not conceiving yet,' I said. 'It will take a few hours if your body accepts my sperm.'

'That what you call it, sperm,' said Love, laughing. 'The archangels call it seed, like you sow in the field. Do you want a baby?'

'I just want to think about it.'

'Oh,' said Love, aghast. 'I thought you loved me?'

'I am, but the baby...?' I said, alarmed. 'Can we talk about it before we make love again?'

'If you want,' said Love, pouting. 'What's there to say?'

'We can talk about it as grown-up adults,' I said. 'I just don't to rush into it.'

'That's fine but you took me anyway,' said Love, disappointed. 'It your responsibility if I'm pregnant.'

'It yours too,' I said.

'You don't want to rush things,' Love said, remorsefully. 'Do you want to make love or not?'

'Yes, I do but not just yet,' I said. 'Why does the archangels procreate but the angels and Christians don't?'

Love got dressed, adjusting her bra. 'You haven't been told? The archangels produce their offspring because they are the highest form of purity.

'Christians are welcome into heaven but they do not have sex but archangels can?' I said, dumbfounded.

'Yes,' said Love, smooching up to me. She took of her bodice and enticing me to come to bed. She spread her wings in a totally submissive way and beckoned to come inside of her.

'Shall we talk about the baby again?' I asked.

'Are you gay?' asked Love, dismayed.

'I am not gay,' I said. 'Just minutes ago we had sex.'

'Several gays often to make love to women,' said Love. 'Are you one of those?'

I tore across the room and bedded my Love, not in a tender way, but ravished her. She was so overcome she yelled out: 'My, you're not gay. You're an animal.'

'But I'm not an animal,' I said, vehemently. 'I'm an archangel.'

'But you are from the earth and before that were an animal,' said Love. 'Archangels born in heaven are pure. You have impure thoughts coming from Earth, but I can save you.'

'No,' I said, 'I'm not impure. I love you.'

'You ravished me,' said Love, accusingly, 'almost raped me!'

'You screamed for more'

Love came over and comforted me with her wings. 'I will teach you.'

'Teach me what?' I asked, inquisitively.
'Love,' said the archangel.

Chapter 56

Love conquers

Archangel Love and I flew out to the island with a giant castle and golden unicorns grazing in the field. There was a pool surrounded by mermaids and peacocks parading in the sun.

As soon as we landed archangel Love invited me into the pool. A host of mermaids joined us. They were playful and enjoying the fun. One of the mermaids held me as I swam and kissed me when I turned at the end of the pool.

Looking on was archangel Love. She turned and walk back to the castle alone. I was wondering if she was jealous, a word rarely used in heaven.

I got to the castle and she was not there. I searched all the rooms and even the butler had not seen her. I went outside and went to the stables and saw Love harnessing the saddle.

'Where have been?' asked Love. 'I'm going for a ride.

'I thought you were you were jealous of the mermaid,' I said, perplexed. 'I thought you were cross.'

'Oh silly,' she said, 'I'm into riding not swimming. 'Saddle up.'

'You saw the mermaid kiss me,' I said. 'You weren't jealous?'

'She's just a mermaid,' said Love, 'I'm an archangel.' With that she rode into the sunset and I chased on my horse.

I raced after her across a meadow and she disappeared into

the woods not knowing if the directions she was taking. I got off the horse and tried to find the tracks she took but to no avail.

Then suddenly out of nowhere Love appeared holding a bouquet of bluebells.

'It's for you, silly,' said Love, giving me the flowers.

'That's nice of you but I was really worried about you,' I said. 'I didn't find your tracks.'

'After I got of the horse I circled the woods by flying over the trees and I saw you and picked the flowers. Come with me and I'll show a little hide-a-away. You'll love it,' she said.

I followed Love into the woods and there was in the distance a log cabin near the lake. Love was in a romantic mood and trying to seduce me.

'When we get to the cabin we'll.......'

'Hush,' said Love, finger over her mouth. 'You will spoil it.'

'Spoil what,' I asked.

'Romance,' said Love. 'That's why here.'

'You said that we could talk about it,' I said.

'Talk about what?'

'The baby,' I said, followed her into the log cabin.

'The baby, the baby... you hadn't even impregnated me yet,' said Love, infuriated.

'That's what I mean,' I said. 'We can talk about it about before we make love.'

'You've said this before,' said Love. 'You just want to talk. Why can't you relax and show me some loving.'

I laid on the bed and look at the surroundings. There were paintings and books and lighted candles and mellow music played softly as Love came over and caressed me.

'There, you can relax now,' said Love, kissing me on the

cheek.

I melted into her arms and she climbed on top and we made love, forgetting about planning babies. Love conquers all. That is why the archangels flourish in paradise.

Sex on earth is bound to suffer whereas the archangels enjoy freedom for their purity. Humans are bound to die because sex and suffering are impure, only Jesus will save them and take them out of suffering and into glory, the eternal home - heaven!

Love gave birth to a dozen archangel babies on Cupid, the same number of Christ's disciples, all of which grew up praising the Lord for His goodness of which I was part of.

Alleluia, Alleluia, Alleluia.

THE END